Loch has chosen to forgo the usual paths that marked men, like him, complete to enter into Service and become fabulously wealthy. He has instead chosen to attend the University of North Carolina. His first year is quite extraordinary as he finds his way and is drawn into a situation with the football team. The team wants to claim him, if not for all of them than at least for one player. Loch finds himself being forced to find a player to date. He finally decides on another freshman, Marcus Battle. Their relationship is just getting started as the school year comes to an end. Neither one of them knows how to negotiate the summer or the next school year. Together they seek the answers to their questions. Will the obvious differences between Marcus and Loch come between them or will they find a way to win the game?

Cageless In College Freshman Year
Copyright © 2020 Crawford Rhine
ISBN: 978-1-4874-3041-2
Cover art by Martine Jardin

Published by eXtasy Books Inc or
Devine Destinies, an imprint of eXtasy Books Inc

Look for us online at:
www.eXtasybooks.com or www.devinedestinies.com

Cageless In College Freshman Year

By

Crawford Rhine

CHAPTER ONE

My first day on campus at the University of North Carolina was a special day. It ranked right up there with the day my baby brother arrived at our house and, of course, the day I received my mark.

The mark resembled a bright blue streak that ran almost from my left earlobe to the tip of my chin. It appeared on the exact moment of my thirteenth birthday. I remember it like it was yesterday. Sitting at the kitchen table with my father, older brother, Paul, younger brother, Stan, and my grandfather, we were talking after just finishing my favorite meal and anticipating the birthday cake.

I saw the look of shock on Dad's face first. It started with a slight widening of his eyes and then followed with the drop of the bottom jaw. Immediately knowing what it was, I ran for the small bathroom near the kitchen. I had been expecting this for quite some time. Flipping on the lights, I quickly looked in the mirror and saw the mark.

The mark was light at first, only a splotch on my cheek, but soon it darkened and got longer. The mark singled me out as a man who was sexually attracted to men. The odds of me receiving a mark were very slim. The mark signaled that I was one of the one percent of men to receive it. I had lived my thirteen years on Earth without ever meeting another marked man or even seeing one in person. Our world contained a majority of non-marked men, who were destined to be sexually frustrated. These non-marked men, or NOMARs, as we call them, are sexually attracted to women, which our world had not contained for hundreds of years.

Several months before the mark actually appeared, I had come to believe that it was imminent. Noticing a change in my body, my mind also started to make the connection that I was more than just friendly with the boys in my class. So, when the mark appeared that night in November, I was not shocked.

My family, however, was stunned. According to my dad, I was the first marked boy in the family for as long as they could remember. I wore my badge proudly, even though my brothers' looks of horror were forever etched in my memory.

School was a bit more of a challenge, but overall, I felt like I had weathered it well. High school was hard enough for most students, but was a special challenge for a student who everyone wanted to fuck.

I had always been a confident person—someone who wasn't afraid to try new things, to speak up in a crowd or to barrel right through a new situation without giving it much thought. But I was not quite ready for the giant pulsing mass of hormones that was my high school years.

Most marked guys chose to forgo most of high school. The mark came with two opportunities. The first one was the chance to go to a Service Academy, which was a special school just for marked guys. Most of the NOMARs referred to these schools as sex academies, since one of the major goals of the SA was to instruct marked men in the erotic arts.

Those lessons usually led to the second opportunity that the mark brought. This was the chance to enter The Service, which was a program where wealthy NOMARs could contract with a marked guy who would become their sexual Servant. The NOMAR would become the Master for the period of a year, and the contract could be extended for more years. In exchange for agreeing to this, the NOMAR agreed to pay the marked man one million dollars for each year of service.

It was a life-changing proposition, one that most marked men could not resist. Wealthy NOMARs also could not resist the notion of having a sex slave at their beck and call every day of the year. However, not every marked man was called. The Service tried their hardest to make the best fit possible, but the marked man had to agree to take whoever they chose as their Master, be he old, ugly, mean, or all of those.

At fifteen, I wanted a normal life, so I decided not to attend The Service Academy. I kept my options open about enrolling in The Service, but I was confident that I could make something of myself either way.

After being relentlessly pursued by multiple boys my first month of high school, I thought it best to get a protector. Always analytical, I decided to go for a senior because I thought it would only last a year and no one would bother to fuck with me with him in the picture. He had to be popular and I wanted him to be handsome and funny. *Was that asking too much?*

It only took a few days once I started looking. I had narrowed it to a member of the basketball team, the wide receiver from the football team, and the student body president. I watched them all in the halls and the cafeteria. I didn't like how cliquey the president was, and the football player, while drop-dead handsome, was not nice to his fellow students who were not on the team.

That left Whitman. He was tall and sleek like a powerful panther. I let him take me to dinner one night and the next day at school, I gave him a blowjob in the empty band room. He had a skinny little cock that was half light pink and half dark pink, like it had been dipped in chocolate.

Two days later, Whitman arranged for me to watch his practice. We lingered in the locker room afterwards until we were the last two left. He seduced me and we fucked for the first time. It was gentle and amazing. I had never felt such pleasure and Whit seemed to really like it, even more than I did.

My plan had worked to perfection. During my freshman year of high school, Whitman and I fucked liked rabbits. Most of the other guys in the school were jealous as hell, but none of them bothered me after that. When Whit graduated, he took a basketball scholarship to a local college and wanted to continue our relationship, but I was done.

Sophomore year, I dated a senior wrestler named West. He was short, thick, and muscled from head to toe. He loved fucking after practice when he was sweaty and smelly. I liked that he fucked me hard and fast, so I didn't care what he smelled like.

Junior year, I had a great time with the quarterback of the football team who told me that he had waited more than two years for his turn with me. Ashton was tall and rangy with a big, muscled chest that he always led with. He was overjoyed that I agreed to be with him and treated me like a prized possession.

Later that year, I was eligible for The Service for the first time, but delayed my enrollment. I was hoping to attend the college of my dreams. My family had always been big fans of the Tarheels and I badly wanted to attend the University of North Carolina at Chapel Hill. I asked for a two-year deferment from The Service, figuring that I would know if I liked college or not after the first year. Marked men always entered The Service, unless they were odd or really unattractive. Going to college was a different path for one of my kind.

Besides, I could always enter The Service at a later time. I told myself that I wasn't missing the golden chance of my lifetime. God, I hoped that I was right! I was very conflicted about what to do with my life, but I was confident that I wanted to go to a regular college before I had to decide. Going to Carolina would give me an excuse to put off making any decision for four years. It was a huge decision to not take the easy path, but one that I was willing to live with for the rest of my life.

I spent my last year of high school with a guy that I had gone to school with for the last twelve years. His name was Chris and he was a musician. He was in a local band and the school band. I loved going to local bars and listening to his band perform. He loved fucking me in front of his band mates while they jammed during practice sessions. Sometimes I would suck them off while Chris was rocking me.

I was elated to get my early acceptance letter to UNC in February. Sometimes it was very helpful to be a member of a minority! I made plans to attend my dream school and enjoyed the last few months of high school with Chris.

CHAPTER TWO

Chapel Hill, the small town where my University was located, was a fantastic environment. UNC was a giant school with NOMARs everywhere. I was assigned to a dorm in the upper quad, which was in the older section of the campus. I had expected a lot of things, but to be a celebrity amongst my fellow freshmen was not one of them. It seems that I was one of just two marked guys to enroll that year on the whole campus, which made me extremely popular with the boys.

Lucky for me, the university had decided to give me a single room while almost everyone else in the dorm had a roommate. I wouldn't have minded either way, but I was glad for the privacy.

Freshmen orientation was a blast. A lot of my fellow students were mature enough to handle a marked guy in their dorm and in their classes, so I didn't have to constantly be on guard. I liked the other freshmen in my dorm and we started to hang out together as a group.

A senior named Chase was my Resident Advisor, or RA, and lived in the middle of my hall. My Freshmen Orientation Counselor was another senior named Matt, who lived on the top floor. Matt encouraged us to go to all of the orientation events and to meet as many people as we could. He said that these connections would last for our entire college career, and the people we met this week would weave in and out of our lives during our four years of college, in classes, at games, at socials, in the dorms, playing intramurals, and eating out.

I took Matt's speech to heart and took my new friends, Bob, Dave, Brandon, and Jeremy with me to all the events. There was a Tuesday night mixer that we attended with a local band headlining, the Cramps. One of the beautiful things about being marked is that guys who normally wouldn't approach a stranger, would approach me to talk about it. So, a lot of guys at the mixer introduced themselves to us and handed us beers.

My friend Dave said that going to a party with me was the best thing ever because the party came to us without us having to do a single thing or buy a single beer. We all laughed about it and had a great time. I constantly scanned the crowd. Being a people watcher, I was fascinated with other people's behaviors, especially when they were drinking.

At some point, I noticed a small group of guys moving through the crowd. They had to be football players, based on their size and the way they were greeted by the other students. They stopped next to us to listen to the band and put down two big coolers that they were carrying. The alpha dogs in the group noticed my mark immediately and made their way over to talk to me.

The jocks were fun to be around, but I was more interested in one of their number who hung back. He had shaggy golden hair and was slightly taller than me at six-foot-three. Shaggy had a great smile and a thick body that hinted at a lot of promise. He never introduced himself like the others in his party, so that made me even more intrigued. I watched him as he laughed with his friends and was amicable with others. I was drawn to him like few guys I had ever met before.

The band ended their set and the football players moved further into the crowd. I watched the one I had nicknamed Shaggy until I lost sight of his group and then turned to see my new friends grinning at me.

"You like 'em big, Loch?" Bob asked with a smirk.

"Yeah, most of the time!" I answered him, laughing.

The boys returned my laughter and Dave introduced me to a friend who was from near my hometown of Charleston, so we had a lot to talk about. Most of the crowd at the mixer was abuzz about the swim test tomorrow.

Carolina had a very odd requirement that all students had to pass a swimming test before they could graduate. Rumor was that a wealthy family at the turn of the century had a daughter at the University who drowned in Jordan Lake and therefore left money for the swimming pool to be built with the stipulation that all students learn to swim.

So, all freshmen took the test during orientation and if they failed, then they spent the next four years trying to pass it. I had an appointment at ten in the morning to take my test. None of my friends were scheduled for their test at the same time as me, so I would go it alone.

I ate a small breakfast in the dining hall the next morning and then walked across the campus down to the natatorium with a pretty large crowd. Ushered into the locker room, my ID was checked and then I was shown a locker. I dressed in a new pair of black and white board shorts that I had bought during the summer to use for this special event.

Upperclassmen ushered us onto the pool deck and put us into lines based on whether we said we were beginners, intermediates, or advanced swimmers. I had always loved the water and my family spent summer vacations at the beach each year, so I moved into the advanced line.

There were about ten guys ahead of me and one in the pool already, so I crossed my arms against the chill of the pool air and waited my turn. The test consisted of swimming a lap and then floating for two minutes. The swimmer in my lane finished floating and climbed out. The next swimmer went in with a splash and I watched as his tanned muscles cut the surface of the water as he free styled.

When the swimmer reached the end wall and began to float, I stepped to the side of the line to watch. This swimmer was big. He displaced a lot of water as he floated. He had short brown hair and a matching brown chin strap beard. His well-formed pecs were covered in the same brown hair, but what really turned me on were his big feet that were completely white on the bottom.

The instructor blew his whistle and the swimmer climbed up the ladder to the pool deck. Someone handed him a towel and I drooled as he dried off his perfectly chiseled body. The instructor signed his swim card and handed it back to him and then almost instantly the swimmer looked directly at me.

Too late! I got caught staring. I looked down way too late and felt my cheeks redden with heat. Not being able to stop myself from looking up, I watched as the swimmer headed for the locker rooms. He was still watching me the entire time he walked across the deck. Our eyes met and my crotch tingled in response.

I could feel the electric burn in my crotch that usually signified the start of a hard-on. Telling myself that he would be gone way before I returned to the locker room, I convinced myself to relax. The last thing I needed was to have a boner when it was my turn to jump into the pool.

The swim test was easy for me, but I was still glad to have it over. I toweled off, grabbed my signed swim card, and headed for the locker room. Going straight to my locker, I figured I would shower off in the dorm and not tempt all of these NOMARs with the sight of my naked ass. I stripped off my shorts and stuffed them in a plastic bag that I had brought with me from the student store. My crotch was still wet, so I used the towel to quickly dry off and that's when I saw him.

Brown chinstrap guy was at the end of my row of lockers. Our eyes met and he headed right for me. He was wearing a frayed pair of camo shorts and a yellow t-shirt that showed off his strapping chest and biceps. Stopping in front of me, he held out his hand.

"I'm Jared." His eyes were a dark caramel-color and reflected the light like polished river rocks.

Do I shake his hand, which would drop my towel on one side and leave myself naked and totally exposed to him? I decided to go with a head nod instead. "Loch," I answered gruffly.

"I watched you swim," he said. "You were really good in the water."

"Thanks. Same to you."

Jared sat down on the wooden bench beside me and continued to scrutinize my body. I wanted to get dressed in a hurry so that if I popped a boner looking at Jared, it wasn't so visible. Quickly dropping my towel, I pulled on my boxer briefs.

"You wanna go up to Franklin Street to grab something to eat for lunch?" Jared asked as I slipped my t-shirt over my head.

"Sure," I said, taking a deep breath. I pulled up my shorts. "You think you might want to fuck afterwards?" I looked straight into his eyes and slipped my feet into my sandals.

Jared's face lit up like it was Christmas morning. "Can we?"

I chuckled at his youthful excitement. "Yes, we can."

We left the natatorium together and started the long walk to Franklin Street. Now that I had put the question on the table, so to speak, Jared was much more relaxed. He had a bounce in his step that I wasn't sure I liked because I considered it cocky. I wondered if he felt that way because he was with me and was going to get laid or whether he walked that way all the time.

Jared talked about how he was going to join a fraternity,

but had not settled on one yet. He told me he was on the football team and how much time all the practices and meetings took. He told me about his hometown of Monroe, right on the North Carolina side of the South Carolina-North Carolina border.

I suggested that we eat at Hector's, which was a local favorite of most students at the university. Taking seats on the counter in front of the plate glass window, Jared ate fast and waved to a lot of people. I couldn't really tell if he was attention seeking or overly friendly.

"We got to get going," Jared said, his voice already raspy with need. "I got practice at one."

"I'm done," I said as I wiped my mouth with my napkin and stood up to throw away my garbage. "Which dorm are you in?"

"Oh, we can't go there. I room in a suite in Ehringhaus with the players."

"I wasn't suggesting that," I said, mildly annoyed. "I was just asking."

"We will have to go to your room," Jared said, completely unscathed by my annoyance.

"No problem, but I don't want to draw attention either, so I'm going to go in first and then you will follow."

"Okay," he mumbled, fazed for the first time by the fact that I didn't want to be seen with him.

We walked the short walk to my dorm and he hung at the edge of the quad.

"Second floor, room two-eleven," I informed him and started to walk.

I had barely gotten the key in the lock when I felt his presence behind me. Jared pressed his body against mine just as I opened the door and fell inside.

Turning around to stare at him, I was about to lay into him when he apologized. "Sorry, I couldn't wait."

I tried hard to be mad at him, but his beautiful smile stopped me in my tracks. Closing and locking the door, I put down my soda from lunch and then he was all over me.

Jared decided to rub his hard cock on me as a first signal of mating.

"Whoa, big fella." I laughed. "You never fuck anyone before outside of a Service Station?"

A Service Station was basically a brothel for NOMARs to go to since they had no sexual outlet in our world. Many men, some marked and some not, worked in the Service Stations, getting fucked and sucking cock for money. It was a necessary evil in our world and no one wanted to wind up working in one of those. At a station, the sex was absolutely anonymous, because the client never saw the man he was fucking or being sucked by, thanks to a thick layer of rubber and a uniquely designed sex chamber.

Many of my marked brethren and I had to deal with NOMARs who had never actually touched or talked to the guys they had sex with before. If we chose to fuck around with these NOMARs, there was usually some awkward moments of education that needed to happen.

"Never," he said in a whispered rush of air.

"Well, this is not how you start, Jared," I told him, chuckling as I pointed to his hard member pressed onto my thigh.

"Sorry," he said quickly and stepped back.

Letting him off the hook, I dropped down to my knees in front of him and said, "Let's see what I'm working with here."

I pulled his cargo shorts down and his stiff cock bounced out towards me right in front of my face. It was a little longer than average with a slight bend in the head that pointed it up somewhat. Overall, it was a good solid dick and I grabbed it in my hand and started playing with it.

Jared's scent was strong and masculine and I inhaled deeply of it. I rubbed his super-soft skin as it slid easily over his steely shaft. He began to leak pre-cum and I used my tongue to catch every drop of it. Already moaning above me, Jared begged me for release.

I accommodated him by gorging myself on his cock. He tasted fantastic, like soap, and sweat, and man. I licked and sucked, hollowing out my cheeks to take long pulls on him. Jared put his hands on my head and started to move it to better suit him.

"Goddamn!" he said to the ceiling as he threw back his head.

Pulling on his nuts, I sucked hard, using my tongue to put pressure on the big vein running along the bottom of his cock from root to head, and heard him groan appreciatively.

"Fuck! I'm coming!" he spat out to me through clenched teeth. Jared held my head in a vise grip with both his hands as he hastily thrust into my mouth over and over. His cum hit the back of my throat in huge spurts. I swallowed it as fast as he could produce it. It was salty and strong and I sucked on his deflating wiener to provoke more beads of cum from his fuck stick.

Jared was speechless as he fell over his climax and then tried to recover from it. I licked my lips and checked my face to make sure I hadn't missed any of his cum as I sat back on my heels.

"That was pretty hot," I said, looking up at the expression of awe on his face.

"Hottest thing I've ever done," he whispered.

"I bet I know of something we can do that will be hotter," I said playfully.

"Oh, I know that your ass is going to be better than your mouth. You are a virgin?"

I looked at him in disbelief. "Did I suck cock like a virgin?"

He flushed slightly and admitted, "No."

"That's right!" I said, chuckling.

13

Chapter Three

Jared and I moved to the bed. I sat on the edge after we had both undressed. Sucking his cock back to a hardened state, I started to fantasize about this big muscular stud being on top of me and I got hard instantly. Jared's body was even better without his clothes, which was rare in my experience. His broad chest was covered with thin brown hair at the top of his pecs and then shaven smooth everywhere else.

"Somebody's ready to go!" Jared said, his voice already deeper than normal with lust.

"You want me to shower the chlorine off me? I smell like you've already shot a load all over me," I said with a chuckle.

"No, let's do this!"

"Let's go, stud!" I said, lying back and pulling my legs to my chest. I grabbed a bottle of lube from my nightstand, squirted a dollop in my hand, and then reached out for his dick.

Jared moved closer until his cock was in my hand. I slicked it up and loved how hot it was to my touch. He was not the longest, nor the thickest, but he was the total package, so I was overly anxious to get started.

Sliding to the edge of my bed, I watched with wide eyes as Jared stepped up to my ass. He hesitated, his eyes never leaving my asshole.

"This is so fucking cool," he said, like a boy with a remote-control helicopter in his hands. He rose up onto his toes and, holding his cock at the base, guided it into me.

It had been a few weeks since my last fuck with Chris, so I

was more than ready for this, but the pleasure and pain of it caught me off guard for a second. I sucked in a deep breath and arched my back as Jared slid that big piece of meat inside me.

"Fuck me!" Jared gasped as my anal ring closed around his shaft and milked his cock down its entire length, as if it had a mind of its own. Jared wasn't as big as some of my former lovers, so I used my ass muscles to squeeze his cock hard as he settled between my legs. His pubic hair tickled my ass when he buried his prick to the nuts in me and he held us steady for a second before he started pumping.

"Hit it hard!" I challenged him.

He smirked at me and then fucking tore my asshole up. Jared fucked me hard and deep with each stroke. I continued to milk his hot cock with each of his out-strokes.

Apparently, Jared knew what to do in the drilling department, because I was soon sweating and holding onto his muscular biceps as he rocked me. The sweat began to run down his chest between his pecs, so I leaned forward and relieved him of it with my mouth as it ran onto his six-pack abs. Just for added measure, I sucked each one of his hard little nipples into my mouth afterwards.

Jared grunted in pain as I sucked his nipples with my hot mouth. He came in a great jerking orgasm that shook me, the bed, and his own body as he filled up my sore hole with his creamy discharge. I continued to ride the wave, fucking myself back and forth on his pole when he had stopped thrusting forward.

The football stud collapsed on top of me, catching himself with his elbows on either side of me before slamming down onto my chest. "Holy shit, that was good!"

"Not bad for a freshman, Jared!" I teased him.

His eyes squinted and he said, "You gonna get with a senior? What am I saying? Of course, you will."

"I usually can put up with someone for about ten months and then I'm done," I admitted honestly.

I saw the cockiness disappear from his demeanor when he very softly asked, "And you wouldn't want to spend it with me?"

"No, but I would be willing to fuck again. You are so fucking hot!" I stroked his ego to soothe him.

A small smile crept back onto his face as he pulled back and out of me. I rolled forward and sucked his cummy cock back into my mouth. I cleaned him off and sucked him back up hard.

"Are you sure I can't keep you?" Jared asked with his eyes closed, driving his cock in and out of my hungry mouth.

"I'm not something to be kept, Jared," I answered after spitting his cock out and massaging it with my hand.

He grunted as I turned away from him, knelt on the bed and held onto the headboard. From this angle I could watch in the mirror hanging on my closet door as Jared fucked me. The small bed creaked as Jared's heavy frame climbed onto it with mine.

"You need me to lube again?" he asked.

I smiled to myself. He was getting more considerate with each fuck. *Maybe I should stay with him!* "No, stud. You filled me up with your hot cream already, so I'm ready to go!"

Jared sidled up behind me and pushed his bent cockhead into my rosebud. I loved the feeling of my asshole opening up and allowing him entrance. He pushed it in even deeper this time as we were basically spooning each other.

"Fuck! I love being inside this ass of yours!" he gushed.

"I love you being in there," I said breathlessly. Watching in the mirror, I couldn't believe that this hot man was fucking me.

Jared plowed a huge furrow in my ass, eventually squeezing my nipples as he rode me like a cowboy on a bucking bull.

It was an impressive display of fucking, especially after just coming twice already. Moaning loud enough to alert my neighbors, Jared rammed into me so hard and deep that it flattened me against the headboard of the bed and the wall.

For the first time since I crawled onto the bed, I was not watching in the reflecting glass but actively engaging in this fuck. That impressed me with Jared and I wondered if I could be happy with him for the first time. Then I remembered his cocky walk and attitude and knew that this fuck would probably be our last.

Jared's climax did not happen quickly this time and his constant thrusting as well as my cock being pushed back and forth against the headboard was more than I could take. I put my head back onto his shoulder and fell over the edge of my climax. Shooting strands of hot cum between my sweaty body and the bed, I felt my ass muscles squeeze even tighter around Jared's cock.

"Fuuuuuuccccckkkkkkk!" he hissed through bared teeth as he buried to the hilt in me and busted his nut again.

We both collapsed onto the bed and tried to catch our breaths.

"Awesome," I eventually said, stroking his side and the top of his perfect hip.

"Incredible," he agreed. "You sure you don't want more of that?"

"Maybe," I laughed. "We do have four years together here!"

"Yeah. It's just the start."

"Want to shower before you go?" I asked.

"Not afraid to be seen with me in the shower?" he asked, chuckling into my back.

"It's the middle of the day. Should be empty," I said sarcastically. Extricating myself from him and his cock, I got us two over-sized towels and my shower caddy. We wrapped the towels around our filthy lower halves and walked to the shared bathroom for my hall. I could feel myself walking funny. My ass was still burning from Jared's constant assault.

Jared went in to shower while I brushed my teeth. I joined him a minute later and saw that Bob and Brandon were both showering. Our dorm was old, so we had a long shower room without curtains or walls between each shower. It allowed you to see everything. Unfortunately, that meant I had to walk past everyone to get to the far end.

Bob and Brandon both turned to me and must have noticed my odd gait. Brandon was the first one to speak, "You get hurt at the swim test today, Loch?"

Fuck! That's why they are showering in the middle of the afternoon. I forgot about that already!

Bob answered for me by saying, "More like he got lucky at the swim test."

I turned on the water and saw the look of enlightenment cross Brandon's face and then he took a hard look at Jared.

"Well look at him, fellas! What was I supposed to do?" I asked loudly as I pointed at Jared's fantastic body.

Jared laughed and I introduced him to two of my new friends. That moment broke the ice even more between me and my friends, and the group of us including Jeremy and Dave, became buddies who could kid each other about anything. The rest of the week flew by with course selection, pep rallies, student store purchases, and seminars on safety, conduct expectations, and technology.

Jared continued to text me daily, but I had not seen him since that day of the swim test. My boys and I decided to celebrate the end of the week with a bar crawl on Franklin Street. None of us were familiar with the different bars, but thought we could see what each of them had going on.

We had been to Linda's and Troll's. They were full of college kids who have returned to campus after the summer break. The students were busy getting re-acquainted. I enjoyed hanging out with my new friends and all the NOMARs watching. I saw a couple of really cute boys, but nothing developed from it.

He's Not Here was the next bar we crawled to. This one had a different feel to it and one that I liked a lot. It had an outdoor area as well as an indoor bar and the crowd seemed to be comprised of locals as well as college students. We grabbed a beer in the iconic He's Not Here plastic cups and found a high-top table to rest against. It was little more than a two by four hanging off a support beam, but it provided a base for us as we talked about the week.

We had only been at this bar for ten minutes or so before I was approached. I felt a hand on my lower back, which was far too familiar for anyone to do to me except my friends.

Turning around, I prepared to shut this kid down. Instead, I turned to my left and was face to face with a man. He was just as tall as me, but much thicker. His blond hair was cut close to his head except at the top of his forehead where it was longer, reminding me of a military haircut.

"Hey man, can I buy you one?" he asked with his voice, but his icy blue eyes implored me for something else entirely. They were slightly bigger than I usually would like, but somehow they fit his face.

I looked at him, a little speechless for a couple of seconds. He was probably thirty years old, wearing a white t-shirt and jeans. Large biceps protruded from his shirt sleeves, one of them covered completely with some type of tattoo. His muscles weren't cut and hard like Jared's, but were more massive.

"You can buy us a round," I said quickly, suddenly aware that there had been an awkward moment of silence while I sized him up.

"Cheers to that!" Jeremy said, raising his cup.

"All right, I'm Tony."

"Hi, Tony," Brandon grinned. The boys had already seen me reject numerous drunk suitors, so they were very excited that I finally let one of them buy us some beers.

"Yeah, hi, Tony!" I laughed. "I'll help you carry the beers," I told him as I turned around. We headed to the bar and placed our order. That gave us a few seconds to talk.

"You in the military?" I asked.

"Cop," he answered.

Hot cop I said to myself.

"You a student?" he asked.

"Freshman."

"Young," Tony said under his breath.

"Old enough for you," I flirted. "How old are you?"

"Just turned thirty."

"Well, happy birthday, Tony," I said to him as I lifted the cup the bartender just handed me. He did the same. "You don't look like a Tony," I said, looking into his eyes.

"Oh, yeah? What would you like to call me?"

"Will you let me call you anything I want?" I teased with a raise of my eyebrow.

"Only if you give me a really good birthday present," he teased back. Tony paid for the beers and we carried them all back to the table.

"Thanks, Tony!" my buddies cheered.

Tony and I stood to the side and continued our flirting. He asked, "So, what name will I go by tonight?"

I eyed him through narrowed lids. "You're pretty confident, aren't you?"

"I am." His broad grin showed me a set of beautiful white teeth.

"I like that in a cop." I laughed. "Not sure yet. I'll think about it."

Tony's white t-shirt was thicker and of a higher quality than most and it looked really good on his tanned skin. I wanted to see his chest through the shirt but was unable to. The veins on his thick neck were driving me wild, so much so that my cock was threatening to show itself off in my shorts.

"What's your tat supposed to be?" I asked.

Tony put his beer down, raised his arm, and pulled his shirt sleeve up. "It's a shield that wrapped around my bicep in front of a background of a glacier and a sea full of icebergs."

"Odd," I said as I touched his arm. The line of his gaze left his tattoo and looked directly into my eyes. His eyes were burning with lust and desire. "But, I like it a lot," I added as I continued to run my fingers around his bicep to see every side. "I understand the shield, since you're a cop, but why the icebergs?"

"My family is from Greenland," he said easily, as if he has had to explain it a hundred times.

"Ah," I said. "Then I will call you my big polar bear to-night." I pointed from his bicep to his white shirt.

"So, I am going to get a birthday present then?"

"Probably, polar bear," I said, unable to stop smiling.

CHAPTER FOUR

I was in my freshmen glory in college—getting the attention of an older man and free beers. Tony bought me and my buddies another round of beers. I let Dave go with him to carry them while I chatted excitedly with the rest of my friends.

Bob asked, "Is he a keeper, Loch?"

"I don't know whether I will keep him, but I might take him home tonight!" I winked.

The boys all laughed and cheered me with their beers.

"He's a cop, so that might come in handy later," I said, trying to justify my whorishness.

"Shit, Loch! You're not worried about fucking a cop when it's illegal?" Dave asked. He had already told us that he was pre-law, so this statement made us all laugh. It was illegal for a NOMAR to fuck a marked guy, unless the marked man was his Servant.

"Cops have cocks too, Dave!" I said, laughing hard. *And I was betting that Tony had a nice fat one.*

We were sitting close to the door, so every time it opened, I got a good look at the new men entering. This time when the door opened, a huge guy walked in. He was tall and thick, at least six-foot-five and over three hundred pounds. He had dirty blond hair that was receding and a full matching beard and stache.

The new stud was wearing a super-tight Under Armour shirt that had been under a football jersey that he had removed and slung over one shoulder. His chest was spectacular under that tight fabric and he had a pretty nice size beer belly — all good in my book.

I looked over at Tony and he was still occupied at the bar. Looking back, I watched the new stud make his way through the crowd gathered at the door. He saw me instantly and I tried to look away, but was too slow. When I looked back he was coming straight towards me.

Now that he was closer, I could see he was older—maybe late thirties. He smelled of cigar smoke and he absentmindedly flexed his huge biceps. His hazel eyes made him look like a guy you would want to party with.

"Hey, buddy."

"Hey, big man."

He grinned crookedly and said, "You wanna get out of here?"

I loved the brashness of this new guy. He was going for it and wasted no time with small talk, but it was confidence driving his actions and not cockiness.

"I got a beer coming," I said, returning his smile. Out of the corner of my eye, I saw Dave and Tony approaching.

"Get the fuck out of here. He's with me!" Tony bristled as soon as he saw the over-sized NOMAR in his territory.

I didn't want a fight, but I did appreciate Tony's instant protection over his investment. I loved a man that was going to fight, if necessary, to be with me.

New guy turned to Tony and said, "He wants a real big cock not that little pencil dick of yours!"

It was one of the worst things he could have said to a man and I knew that Tony would throw a punch, so I prepared for it. But, instead, both big men burst out laughing and hugged each other.

"Seriously, Bo, you need to get lost." Tony laughed. "Loch, this is my buddy, Boone."

"Nice to meet you, Boone. These are my buddies," I said

with a wave of my hand and introduced my friends. I handed Boone my beer, feeling that I was going to need all my wits about me tonight. Not a heavy drinker, I was always cautious about drinking. The last thing I wanted or needed was to get drunk and make bad choices in a bar full of horny NOMARs.

Tony made sure he stood behind me as he talked to Boone and very possessively put his thick hand on my shoulder.

I countered this by saying, "I gotta take a piss."

Jeremy jumped up to go with me. My new friends had already learned never to let me go anywhere alone in a crowd like this and that's why I liked them so much.

After using the facilities, Jeremy and I were washing our hands when he looked at me in the mirror and asked, "So, which one is it going to be, Loch?"

I smiled at him and said, "Am I that obvious?"

"Yeah." He grinned back at me. "You get real focused on the guy when you are attracted to him."

Laughing, I said, "Good to know." Throwing some paper towels at my new friend, I put him in a headlock as we left the restroom. I got a lot of stares from hungry college kids and sauced locals as I walked through the bar and back outside.

Boone and Tony had stepped to the side of our table and were deep in conversation. Both sets of eyes followed me as I rejoined my buddies, despite the intense conversation they were having. Normally that would make me feel like I was a piece of meat, but tonight I wanted to be spit roasted like the giant piece of man meat that I was.

"I'll see you boys in the morning—or the afternoon," I said with a laugh to my friends at the table. "We're going to see *Gone Girl* at the matinee tomorrow, right?"

Bob shook his head and shoulders and said, "You are the only person I know who is about to fuck around that is level-headed enough to be making your plans for tomorrow!"

Everyone laughed, causing my two studs to look our way.

"I hope I can sit tomorrow, Bob, but it is good to know that it's going to be a padded movie theater seat and not one of those wooden seats in class!" I tossed out as I held my hand up, waving goodbye.

I walked over to Boone and Tony and said, "Let's go!"

Tony looked shocked and said, "Which one of us?"

I smiled at Tony and ran my hand over his bristly crew cut. "You're definitely coming, polar bear." Turning to Boone, I ran my hand over his thick golden beard. "But, we might need a grizzly bear also."

"Both of us?" Boone asked in surprise.

"Either of you got a problem with that?" I challenged. I knew neither of them would risk blowing the deal to complain.

Tony looked at Boone with a raised eyebrow. Boone just shook his head slightly from side to side.

"I'm going to fucking treat you both like kings!" I smirked. I saw their eyes glaze over with lust. Starting to walk towards the door, I gave them a good view of my ass as an appetizer.

Once outside on the sidewalk, I asked, "Any ideas where we can go?"

"I live nearby in an apartment," Tony said.

"Works for me," Boone agreed.

"Let's go!" I said. Boone offered to drive and led us to an enormous truck with huge tires covered in mud.

"I hope you are not compensating for a small dick, Boone!" I smirked, indicating the size of the truck.

"You'll see!" He winked and helped me up into the cab, which was almost as large as a small car. Tony climbed up into the passenger seat and we took off.

Extending both of my hands to the boys' crotches, I was rewarded with the outlines of both of their hard cocks. I rubbed them through their jeans and then dropped myself to the floorboard and twisted around.

Tony's fly came down easily so I reached in and carefully extricated his large cock. It was a beautiful dick, long and wide with beautiful pale white skin and I went down on it immediately. It tasted like sweat and soap and I licked all the way down the shaft, putting my tongue into the fly of his jeans. I had my other hand, meanwhile, continuing to stroke Boone's big cock through his jeans.

My new cop friend put his head back on the seat and moaned as I teased his piss hole with the tip of my tongue and sucked on his cock head. Pulling off of him, I used my hand to continue to put pressure on the big vein underneath his shaft while I turned my attention to his friend.

Boone's cock was a bit more difficult to pull through his fly, either because of the steering wheel being in the way or his exceptional length. His fire hose was unbelievably long with thick veins running up and down its entire shaft, reminding me of a French tickler. It wasn't as thick as Tony's and in even more contrast to his, was a deep red color.

Wrapping my lips around the long cock in front of me, I tasted sweat and the unmistakable musk that comes from a man that has already climaxed. He must have jerked off before he came out to the bar. His crotch smelled of cigar smoke and it occurred to me that it was strange that his truck didn't.

I worked back and forth between the two studs until we arrived at Tony's place. They awkwardly zipped up before we walked to the upstairs apartment where Tony let us inside. It was a nice little apartment, but Tony didn't even turn the lights on as he led us to the back bedroom.

Happy to see a queen-sized bed in Tony's bedroom, I was relieved that the three of us big guys weren't going to be crammed on a small bed.

"Lights on or off?" Tony asked.

"I wanna see you two bucks go at me," I smirked.

"Fair enough," Tony growled. "If it's anything like that

fucking blowjob you started to give us in the truck, then you can have anything you want, Loch."

I usually get what I want anyway! I stripped in front of these two NOMAR friends. I went slow, giving them a good show and letting them get the full shot of my ass as I leaned over to take off my jock.

Boone and Tony stripped in a heartbeat. Their cocks were so hard they looked as if they might not be restrained by their skin sheaths. Dropping to my knees onto the carpet, I ran my hands over both of their meaty butts before taking turns consuming their pricks. I watched them carefully as I enjoyed sucking one meat missile and then switching to the other.

Tony's body was dense and strong. He was almost completely hairless, having shaved his chest and crotch. I could see fine blond hairs under his arms, but those were the only ones I could see. Running my hands over his solid backside, I could feel the small hairs that he had not shaved.

Boone's body, in contrast to his friend's, was muscled and cut. His chest was full of his golden blond hair and his protruding beer belly was covered with it as well. He had not bothered to manscape his pubic hair and there was an extensive amount of it.

My mouth was full of Tony's thick girth when I heard Boone reach inside his pants and hand something to Tony. Looking up around his cock, I saw that it was a cigar being passed between them. Boone lit both stogies and all three of us took long drawing pulls from our sticks.

Already feeling like I was being incredibly naughty, it was taken to a new level of hotness by them smoking while they fucked with me. I had never been in a three-way before and I had never been fucked by someone twice my age. These were real men, the kind my father had always taught me to avoid, because they would take advantage of me and use me. At the moment, I felt like I was the one doing both to them.

Tony and Boone were both starting to leak a large amount of pre-cum. I took turns licking and sucking it out of their hard units. The man-honey had an intoxicating effect on me and I couldn't get enough of it.

Pulling Boone's long prick out of my mouth, I stood up and asked, "Tony, you ready to get your birthday present?

"I thought I just was . . ."

"I've got a hole that's even hotter and tighter for you," I said, leering as I crawled up onto the bed on all fours. I had already scoped out the bedroom and seen the full mirrors on the closet doors, so I knew that I could watch my big polar bear while he fucked me from this position.

"I bet you do," Tony's deep voice rumbled. He disappeared into the bathroom and emerged with a squirt bottle of lube. I watched in the mirror as he lubed his cock and then squirted a dollop on the top of my crack.

"Happy birthday, buddy." Boone's rough fingers followed the lube down to my hole before he pushed two of them inside me. "Oh, he's so fucking hot and tight." He finger-blasted me back and forth to get me ready. "He's going to be amazing!"

Tony climbed into the saddle behind me, Boone removed his fingers, and I braced my arms against the mattress. My polar bear pushed his tasty cock against my puckered hole and split my anal ring. The hot cop sank into me and then growled with pleasure.

I was fucked so hard by the policeman that my arms collapsed and my head hit the mattress. My face was smashed, but I was still able to see Tony plowing a wide furrow in my ass. I was soon distracted by Boone standing on the side of the bed and feeding his long cock into my mouth.

It was the first time that I had ever had two cocks inside me at the same time and it was a wonderful moment. I had always thought that I would be way too distracted by one cock to notice the second one, but I had been wrong. I could totally feel my asshole squeezing Tony's big member, even while my tongue was swiping more pre-cum from Boone's piss slit.

"Shhhhhiiiiiitttttt! I'm coming inside your tight hole!" Tony groaned, his cigar clenched between his teeth.

"Fill it up, Tony!" Boone encouraged his friend, blowing smoke over my ass.

Tony did just that—filling me with his hot seed. He slowly came back to himself after his release, still thrusting back and forth slowly.

"Trade places with me, Bo," Tony said, pulling his sloppy cock out of my ass and flipping me onto my back.

Boone lifted my ass off of the bed and spread my legs. I wasn't sure what he was doing at first, but it was thrilling to me to be manipulated by this big man. My grizzled man kept lifting my legs until I was upside down on my neck. Tony held me while Boone used his hands to split my ass cheeks and looked at my puckered hole.

"Small little thing," he commented, almost to himself. He took a long pull on his cigar and then used his fingers to stretch my hole open. Putting his face right into my crack, he blew the hot cigar smoke directly into my anal channel.

I was instantly heated from the inside out. The grizzly bear pulled my legs up onto his broad shoulders and bent me in half. He fed his long tool into my sore hole and started to undulate his body on top of me, driving that nine-inch dick into me over and over again.

"This hole is so fucking hungry for cock," Boone moaned as he fucked me.

Tony squatted over my face and slid his cummy cock into my mouth. It was totally hot cleaning polar bear's cock right after he had fucked me with it. When I finally had his prick clean, Tony backed off and Boone lay down further onto me. His hairy belly was stimulating my erection with each stroke and soon I wasn't able to hold it in.

"Fucking me deep, grizzly bear!" I yelled. "Fucking the cum right out of me."

Grunting hard, I fell over the edge of my climax and shot my load between our stomachs and chests. With each of Boone's deep thrusts, he pounded more hot cum from my cock.

Boone wasn't far behind, growling as he filled me with his steaming seed. My two bears spent the next two hours filling all of my holes as many times as their bodies would allow them. When they collapsed in exhaustion, I think I had already fallen asleep. The three of us woke early the next morning in a sticky, stinky pile. It was one of the most fantastic nights of my life!

CHAPTER FIVE

After my first *ménage-a-trois* I found it hard to sit down for close to three days. At first, I thought that I might have done some damage to my poor little asshole, but the thought of going to the campus clinic and asking about it was horrifying to me. I was so happy when my backside started to feel better.

Classes had started and I was thrilled with them. There was a lot of work, but most of it was exciting. I got a text from Jared while I sat in class on Wednesday.

Hey Loch, can't stop thinking about our day after the swim test.
It was a good day!
Wanna do it again?
I thought we talked about that.
We did, but you can't blame me for trying, can you?
I guess not.
Wanna go to a party this Saturday?
No strings . . .
What kind of party?
Football party. An alumnus in the NFL rented us a house off campus.
Not sure.
You can invite your boys. Honest, I won't bother you.
Okay. I'll ask them and if they want to go, I'll be there.
Awesome. I'll text you the info.

This whole string worried me a little bit. Jared had never been anything but honest and respectful, but I didn't want to lead him on. What really bothered me was the fact that I loved being fucked by him, but I knew that there was no future there for us. I was afraid that I was sending him the wrong signals, so I was probably harsher with him than I should have been.

After class, I met my friends in the lounge of the dorm and told them about Jared's offer.

"Their parties are epic!" Bob said with excitement.

Jeremy agreed. "Plus, think of the cred we will have after attending."

Dave had been quiet for a while. He looked at me now and asked, "Do you think it is safe for you to go, Loch?"

"Well, obviously, there is only one thing that they want," I said with a shrug of my shoulders. "I think that having you guys there will be the buffer that I need. I won't go without you."

"We wouldn't let you go without us." Brandon snorted.

"So, it's settled? We have a party to go to this weekend?" Jeremy asked, barely able to contain himself.

"Absolutely!" I said, high-fiving all of my friends.

"I've heard that sometimes they have marked guys from the local Service station at their parties. No offense, Loch," Brandon said.

"None taken," I said, starting to laugh. I was sure that constantly being around me without any sexual release was frustrating for my new friends and if they could get their rocks off at this party, I was all for it. They had been very good to me in the short amount of time that I had known them and I would be so happy for them to get something in return, in addition to my friendship.

I had a big test on Friday, so I spent the rest of the week preparing for it. Friday came quickly and I did well on my Spanish test, so I was on top of the world. As I walked back to my dorm, it hit me like a bolt of lightning that I was horny as hell. I hadn't realized while I was studying or taking the test, but now my ass was itching and my balls were tingling with lust.

Jared was so excited that I was coming to the party tonight and continued to blow up my phone about it. Boone and Tony had also been texting. I was suddenly very popular, but in my brain there was some part that knew I was on the wrong course. My behavior so far since I arrived on campus, while a shit load of fun, had been dangerous.

NOMARs get worked into a frenzy by a marked man's attention and I was poking the bear. I had always been a one-man kind of boyfriend and I knew that this was the way I wanted to go now, at least for a year. I had a pattern and one year was usually my limit before I got bored. I didn't see why this formula wouldn't work for me now.

My friends were totally excited about the party and we ordered two pizzas to be delivered while we played cards and listened to music to pass the time. Word had gotten out about us being invited to the football team's party and our social standing had immediately been elevated because of it.

Wanting to be a little late, we left for the party at nine o'clock. It was at one of the old mansions off of Franklin Street towards Hillsborough, so we could walk there in ten minutes or so. All of us had dressed for what we thought was the occasion with khaki shorts, plaid button-downs, and flip-flops. We looked like a group of frat boys out on the town.

We could hear the party before we could actually see it. As we traversed down the darkened residential street, the noise of a band playing rock and of a lot of people talking loudly reached our ears. Following the noise, I saw a stately old mansion that looked perfectly normal from the front. The noise told a different story.

Dave stepped up and rang the bell, but there was no

answer. Trying the knob, he pushed the door open and we stepped inside. The inside was trashed already. There was no furniture except for old couches, and blue Solo cups and beer bottles were everywhere. A few people were milling about, talking, and when they saw us, they pointed to the back of the house and said, "Everyone's out back. Kegs are in the kitchen."

I led the way to the kitchen door and pushed it open. There were probably twenty or so big guys in the kitchen and most of them went quiet when I stepped inside. I suddenly felt very out of place.

"Who's hogging the beer?" I asked quickly to break the tension. Several guys moved to the side and let us see the kegs. There were three different types of beer and not the cheap stuff that I would have suspected they would have had at these parties.

"Be our guest," one guy said as he put his arm around my shoulders and guided me to the kegs. His breath stank of beer and soon his big hand had slid down to my butt.

"Hands to yourself, buddy!" I said firmly as I wiggled out of his grasp.

My boys closely followed me and we all got a cup of beer. The back door opened and Jared rushed into the room. He was shirtless, showing us all what a fantastic physique he had. "Lodge wants everyone outside!" he said loudly. Jared saw me and stopped in his tracks.

"Loch!" he yelled, holding up his cup.

"Jared!" I cheered back to him. I could tell that he had already had too much to drink.

"Hey, come on guys, QB is about to unveil a surprise!"

Everyone began to file out the back door. Stepping out onto a small landing, I saw that there were a few stairs in front of me and then the backyard opened out onto a pool deck with a rather large pool and a patio sitting area. There were football players everywhere, including in the pool. Standing on top of a brick enclosure for a grill was Daniel Lodge, the quarterback of the team.

Everyone got quiet and he addressed the hoard of boy-men. "Gladiators, tonight we celebrate the start to another great year of Carolina football!"

The crowd cheered wildly.

Lodge continued, "We want to thank our generous alumni for this awesome house and party!" He raised his cup towards a group of older men sitting at a patio table.

The crowd cheered and hooted their appreciation.

"And for our special surprise tonight!" As he talked, several football players pulled back a huge curtain and revealed one of those portable tents. From inside the tent came a mysterious smoke-swirling in a Carolina blue light.

Fascinated by this whole spectacle, I leaned forward to try to see inside the tent as did everyone else, but I couldn't see a thing.

"Welcome to the Tar Hole!" Daniel Lodge bellowed and the crowd went berserk.

Jared was on my hip. He leaned into my ear and said, "It's a glory hole. Me and the other freshmen players had to help build it."

I turned around to look at him and I couldn't help but catch his excitement. We both laughed out loud. Dave, Jeremy, Bob, and Brandon were speechless—bug-eyed and speechless.

A guy was soon pressing his cock between my buns. He leaned down and said in a drunk and husky voice, "I won't need a glory hole when I got my big cock buried in this sweet hole."

"Back off, Miller," Jared growled.

"You can't tell me what to do, fish!"

"We can!" Jeremy said, and all six of my friends got between me and the drunk football player. The big player looked at them for a few seconds like he thought maybe he could take them on, but then he backed off and stumbled into the kitchen.

"Thanks, fellas." I sighed. "Let's go down to the pool deck." There were more kegs of beer out here, so we were able to refill our cups.

"Hey, kid, come over here."

I turned to see who had raised their voice and was calling me. It was the group of alumni. Jared had been called away by one of the older players to do some work, so Bob, Brandon, Jeremy, Dave and I walked over to the table where the former players were sitting.

"Hey, kid, what's your name?" a bald guy asked me.

"Loch. And you?"

The older athletes snickered. "I'm Tom. Boy, you got some balls coming in here."

"You think?" I smirked. I took the time to get a good look at these alumni. They were big, burly football types who your heart kinda went out to, because it seemed that they had nothing else in their lives but the game. Now that they were older, they seemed to be still trying to recapture that glory by hanging around the younger athletes.

"In my years here, if a fine marked guy like you would have come to one of these parties, you would have been gang-fucked all night long and probably wound up in a wheelchair for the next month."

"One can only hope," I said as I laughed.

"Oh, you're a smartass and you got a ton of confidence. I can see that now and you were smart to bring your boys with you, but man I still think you got big brass balls for walking in here."

"How about my big brass ones park it over here with you big lunks for a while so that my boys can go experience the glory hole?" I asked. Seeing the looks of shock on my friend's faces, I beamed a huge grin in their direction.

"You need some protection?" a hunky stud with dirty blond hair asked gruffly.

"I do," I easily admitted.

"Deal!" the bald guy said with a toothy grin.

I turned to my boys and said, "Have a great time fellas! I'll be here when you're done."

"You sure, Loch?" Bob asked.

"Absolutely."

My boys high-fived each other as they headed for the tent with the Carolina blue smoke coming out of it. I looked around for a place to sit and not finding any, I looked back up at the older men in the circle.

"Come sit on daddy's lap," a guy with white in his Fu Manchu moustache said to me while patting his thigh.

"Is daddy going to keep his hands to himself?" I asked with a smirk.

"Maybe," he laughed. The gathering roared with laughter.

"All right!" I said back, starting to laugh. Climbing over the other alumni to him, I took a seat on his legs and leaned back off to the side, so I didn't block his view of the party.

Daddy held me in place with an arm around my side. "You didn't want to go to the tent and get off?" he asked in a grizzled voice.

"I have just as good of a chance to get off right here, sitting on this big log," I told him as I reached down and felt his stiff joint through his jeans. I knew I was playing with fire, but something told me that this was the way to win this group of men over.

His friends all laughed and soon we were playing a drinking game where every time anyone said the word *beer*, we had to take a drink. And if anyone asked a question, they had to finish their beer no matter how much was left. I was the mandatory beer fetcher when someone's cup ran dry. I liked hanging out with these guys and found them very funny. They enjoyed telling me stories about their playing days and their time in the NFL.

A couple of drunk football players would wander over and be instantly jealous of me sitting on daddy's lap, but the older men just told them to fuck off and they would quickly leave.

Looking around at all of the players here, it occurred to me that I had not seen the player from the concert last week with the shaggy golden-brown hair. I continued to scan the crowd for him, but when I came up blank, I decided to ask. "So, are all the football players here?"

"Ah! You asked a question. Drink up, Loch." Daddy laughed and bounced me on his lap like I was a kid.

I downed the whole cup of beer as the bald guy pushed the bottom of my cup up into the air. The beer flowed faster than I could swallow, so it soon streamed down my face on both sides, coating my shirt.

"Just like if he was sucking my big hose," Baldy chuckled. "My spooge would be running down the sides of his mouth the same way."

"Yeah, right," Daddy said with a snort. "Loch asked us a question, I believe."

"They are not all here. Some of them have a big test tomorrow, so they are studying with the team tutors," a third guy with bad acne on his round face told me. "We only know that because a lot of them were the team fishes that were supposed to set up for the party and we wound up doing it instead."

"Interesting," I mumbled to myself. I had hoped to see the shaggy haired kid again and see what he was like, but it was not to be. I was pulled out of my thoughts by seeing the QB climb back onto the grilling unit.

"Attention, you horny fucks!" he yelled. When he had everyone's attention, he said, "I suppose by now you have all had the chance to leer at our special guest tonight." With a wave of his hand, he indicated where I was sitting on daddy's lap.

Holding my breath, I froze in place.

"Our special guest's name is Loch and someone here to-night is going to tap that sweet ass!" Lodge yelled.

CHAPTER SIX

I was suddenly put on the spot and I didn't like it one bit. I saw my friends emerge from the Tar Hole slowly to see what the commotion was all about.

Daniel Lodge, the quarterback from the football team, stood on the top of the grilling enclosure and was yelling at the crowd. "Loch here has already been nailed by one of our team!"

A roar went up from the crowd and I caught Jared's eyes from across the pool deck. He had the polite manners to look ashamed and hung his head. I had no qualms about telling people about my indulgences, but I didn't think telling the whole football team was right.

"The fish, Jared, says that he has never felt an ass so tight or sweet before!"

Another roar went up from the crowd. Lodge was inciting a riot and I didn't like it one little bit. Daddy held onto me tightly, sensing my sudden fear.

"So, Loch, tell us. Which one of us is it going to be?" There was silence and then he added, "Or which ones of us will it be? We are a team, after all!"

The crowd yelled again and then there was silence as everyone waited for my reply. Even the alumni were looking at me expectantly.

I needed to shut this down. I prepared to raise my voice and firmly yelled out, "There won't be any of you getting to fuck me tonight."

A chorus of boos erupted from the gathering crowd. The

players from inside the house had now come out onto the pool deck to witness the spectacle.

"Why not? You've already proven that you like to get railed out by the large cocks of the football team!"

There was another huge cheer from the crowd and another glare from me to Jared.

"It wouldn't be fair for me to choose one of you tonight!" I yelled back.

"Why not?" Lodge yelled back. "The football players are the studs on campus and we claim you in the name of our program. Every marked student that attends Carolina gets a football stud's big cock planted inside them!"

Another huge roar went up from the crowd and some of the players eyes started to glaze over as they stared at me. I knew that I had to get out of here quickly.

"I'm not saying that I also won't be joining that elite fraternity, but that it's not fair for me to have to pick someone when the whole team is not gathered here for me to pick from."

"Oh, I see. You want a better selection!"

"I want the whole team, yes!"

"Well, then, we can just get this taken care of after practice on Monday!"

The crowd cheered again.

"That would be acceptable to me, Lodge," I yelled back, "with one stipulation."

"Oh, yeah? Okay, let's hear it."

"I will do as you ask on Monday as long as during this process and then afterwards, the players treat me with respect and accept my decision. That means that I don't want to have to constantly fight off their advances."

"Very good." Lodge turned and addressed the crowd. "Well, boys, looks like the only ones of us getting that ass tonight are the alumni, but our turn will come soon! And Loch is off limits until he makes his selection."

Half of the crowd yelled and the other half groaned before they started to dissipate as the QB jumped down off of the grill.

"Nicely handled," bad acne guy said with a nod of his head.

"Thanks, boys," I said with a wink. "It was easier to make demands with you guys having my back."

My friends made their way over to the patio table and wanted to know what the hell that was about. A group of the alumni had gone to take a piss, but bald guy and daddy stayed with me.

"Just the team asking me to pay for the price of admission to this party," I answered them. "How was the Tar Hole?"

"Fucking amazing!" Jeremy said excitedly.

"That's because he blew his load twice!" Dave said starting to laugh.

"Twice?" I asked with my hands slapped on the side of my face like that famous scene from *Home Alone*.

"I was excited," Jeremy said, defending himself.

"It was awesome!" Bob said in a super high voice. "I got a hand job, a blow job, and got to fuck a pretty decent ass."

"Nice job," I said, high-fiving Bob and then looking at my hand. "Did you wash these afterwards?"

Brandon licked his lips and said, "We're going to get a beer, wash our hands, and then we'll be right back. You need anything, Loch?"

"No, I'm good."

As soon as my boys were out of earshot, I reached over to Baldy's lap and grabbed his hard cock in my hand. Daddy's was under me and I reached for it, as well. Once I had their attentions, I said, "I don't want my boys to know, but if you two only come to my room tonight, I'll fucking give you all the tight sweet boy ass you could ever want."

I enjoyed their looks of shock and then added, "Manly two-twelve."

"No shitting?" Daddy asked.

"No shitting, Daddy. I just rode your hard-on for close to an hour, but tonight I want it planted all the way inside of me." I knew my words were just adding fuel to the fire already burning inside them, but I didn't care. They had done a good job of protecting me and making me feel comfortable, so they deserved a reward. And the fact that Daddy could stay hard for over an hour meant I was going to be in heaven.

Without even looking over my shoulder, I joined my friends at the kegs. We each got another drink and headed home. I didn't want to run into Jared at all and fortunately we didn't. We made it out of there without any further problems and talked about it all the way home. My friends were so happy that they had gotten a piece of tail at the Tar Hole that they were on cloud nine. I felt a little left out as they all talked animatedly about their experiences, but I knew that I was going to get mine tonight.

As soon as we reached our dorm, we said goodnight and headed to our rooms. Most of the boys wanted to take a shower before going to sleep. I was sweaty, but needed to wait for my nighttime visitors, so I sat down and watched a rerun of *Friends* on late night TV.

I heard Daddy and Baldy at the front door to the dorm around two in the morning. They were knocking, since they had no way to get in. I walked down and opened the door for them before they woke everyone up.

"Hey guys," I said, with a finger over my lips.

"Loch." Daddy practically drooled.

I led the aging footballers up to my room and locked the door behind them after they entered. "I don't want you to say a word," I told them as I turned off the lights. Making my way across my small dorm room, I pulled on the blinds over the two windows and made them retract. The moon was low in the night sky and beautifully illuminated my room. I could see clearly.

Walking over to my two new friends, I dropped to my knees in front of them and began to work their shorts down off of their hips. They both helped me with that, and in no time I had their hot dicks in my hand. It occurred to me when I gorged myself on Daddy's dick that I didn't know either of these guys' names.

Oh well, they were just a distraction until Monday and I probably would never see them again. I swapped to Baldy's big drooling member. They didn't have far to go to get rock hard and soon I was spread eagled on my bed and the boys were taking turns pounding my pud like it was the target of the strong man game at a carnival and they were the sledgehammers.

I liked that neither of them spoke as I had told them not to, which left me time to think about Monday's dilemma. Lying on my bed, I was enjoying the pleasure these two older men were giving me, but my brain was working overtime on what I thought was going to happen after football practice in two days.

When Daddy flipped me over onto my back and pulled my ass to the edge of the bed, I knew he was serious. He placed my feet flat on his broad chest and bent me in half. He fucked me so hard, all the while staring into my eyes. When he came, he closed his eyes, arched his back and let out a huge low rumbling growl that vibrated through the room.

Not to be outdone, Baldy fucked me in the same position and busted his nut into my already full chute. I sucked them both up hard again and they spit-roasted me on all fours until they both came again. I let them lie down on the bed on their sides and I slept between them.

We woke early the next morning when the sun rose because we had left the blinds up. I showed my appreciation by blowing both of their morning boners. I let Baldy have his fantasy of watching his cum run out of the sides of my mouth after he came. Both men dressed and left after thanking me. They left me their cell numbers which I promptly threw away.

I was sore and tired, but managed to drag myself to the shower. Dave was also in there and when he saw me, he looked at me with a discerning eye and asked, "You get a late-night booty call, Loch?"

"Yeah." I chuckled.

"Good for you," he said, turning back towards the shower. "I'm still high off of that party last night myself."

"It was a great night," I said with a laugh.

Once everyone was up, we walked uptown to get a greasy breakfast. While we were eating, the boys wanted to know what my plan was for Monday.

"I'm not sure," I told them.

"What do they want, exactly?" Bob asked.

"I'm not sure, but I think it is a pride thing. They want to claim me."

Brandon looked confused. "How?"

"They said that all marked guys get fucked by the team. I think they want me to have one of them as a regular guy that I fuck with."

"Or they want you to be the team pump," Jeremy said, with a note of horror in his voice.

"Or that," I agreed.

Bob asked, "So, they want you to have a boyfriend basically and they want it to be one of them."

"I think so."

Dave raised an eyebrow at me and asked, "Is that something you would want, Loch?"

"Well, I'm not going to just have a boyfriend because they tell me to, but if I like one of them, then I'm not opposed to it. I always had a boyfriend in high school, mostly for protection, but I usually enjoyed it."

"What was his name?"

"I always dated a senior, so I had four different boyfriends during high school," I answered. "I know, it makes me a total slut, but that's the way that I kept the other boys and teachers off of me."

Jeremy shook his head. "You have so much more to worry about than we ever did. I was always worried about looking cool and getting into the popular group. You were worried about your safety."

"Don't make me out to be a saint, Jeremy." I chuckled. "I was getting laid the whole time by four different NOMARs who were horny as hell. This start to school where I have fucked around with several different people is new to me, so if there is a player on Monday that strikes my fancy, I proba-bly would let him be my boyfriend."

"They are going to pressure you for that outcome," Dave surmised.

"Probably," I agreed, taking another bite of toast.

We didn't talk about it again until after classes on Monday.

CHAPTER SEVEN

Football practice ended at six o'clock on Monday and my last class had ended at two, so I had four hours to fret about what was to come. Daniel Lodge had sent me several texts telling me what time, which door I was supposed to enter at Kenan Stadium, and whom I was supposed to ask for entry. He must have gotten my cell phone number from Jared, because I had not given it to him.

I had formulated a plan, but I didn't know if it would work, so I jumped on my computer and started researching. I needed to know as much about each of the players as possible, their criminal pasts, their Facebook activities, their profiles on social media, their families, and just for kicks their potential to play in the NFL, according to the experts. I read the media guide and cyber-stalked each player like a professional detective.

By five forty-five, I was ready to go. I had dressed casually in over-sized basketball shorts and a UNC t-shirt. This outfit managed to cover my body in hopes of not exciting the players too much. My friends had all silently gathered one-by-one in my room.

"So, what's the plan, Loch?" Dave asked.

"You want us to go with you?" Jeremy asked.

"I would love that, but I think I should handle this on my own. Thanks, though." They were really good friends in such a short amount of time and I was more grateful for them than they would ever know.

"Don't let them do anything there in the locker room, Loch,

or it will be a frenzy like at the party," Brandon warned.

"Oh, I know. I don't plan on anything happening today. You guys have been great. I'm really lucky to have you as friends. I'm going to have our text thread pulled up on my phone and if I need help, I will send out an SOS."

My friends circled up and gave me a big hug before I headed out.

It was a little bit of a walk to the stadium, but I used the time to practice what I was going to say. It was a beautiful sunny day and soon I was sweating from the humidity and sun. By the time I got to the stadium, I was starting to have swamp-ass. I followed Lodge's directions and a stadium employee escorted me to the home locker room.

I was so interested in seeing the internal parts of the stadium that I didn't even realize when we had arrived at the locker room. The employee held the door for me as I stepped inside. He closed the door just as a waft of sweat and musk hit my nose like a brick wall.

Walking down a short hallway, I emerged into the locker room. The boys were all standing facing me like statues, most of them having stripped off their practice jerseys and a few were even in only jock straps. It was an amazing display of masculinity that reminded me of the Terracotta Army of China.

Daniel Lodge emerged from the crowd and said loudly, "Loch, welcome!"

He shook my hand as I said, "Thanks."

"So, here is the whole team as you requested," Daniel said, with a gesture of his hand.

I looked out over the crowd of ninety or so players. It was overwhelming. Noticing right away that the seniors were in the front line, I assumed that they had arranged themselves by class.

"The boys are a little upset with me that I suggested we do this now, because they don't look . . . or smell their best after practice."

"I prefer it that way," I immediately answered.

Daniel chuckled and asked, "So, how will this work?"

I looked at him hard to see if he could be trusted to keep his word or not. I decided that he could. "Well, I think I will pick a few players who I would like to get to know better and then we can go out this week. If one of them is worthy, then I will . . ."

"Will what?" Lodge's eyes gleamed with delight.

"I will spend more time with him."

Lodge smiled and asked, "You will pick one of them as your boyfriend?"

"Yes."

"And if none of them are worthy?"

"Then we go about our separate ways, I guess."

Daniel Lodge quickly corrected me. "No, we will start over. If you do not like any of them, then we will reconvene next Monday after practice and you will pick more of my brothers to date."

I swallowed hard, now knowing for sure that I was not getting out of this. "Okay."

He smiled and said, "Excellent! Start shopping." He fell into the first line.

It took me a few seconds to decide how I was going to approach this. I started weaving in and out of the line of seniors. I watched with delight as they sucked in their stomachs and flexed their muscles for me. The smell was sour, but I found myself getting turned on anyway. Deciding to get a good look at everyone before making any decisions, I walked in and out of the lines. The players purposely made it so that I would have to touch them to squeeze between them.

Finishing the line of seniors and juniors, I did the same

thing to the sophomores and freshmen. I saw Jared right away but he would not meet my eyes. Passing him by, I was fearful that my shaggy guy wasn't there, but I saw him towards the end of the line. He looked into my eyes and then immediately down at the floor. I felt some kind of pull with him that I had never experienced before, but I had no idea why or what it was.

Moving back up to the free area in front of the seniors, I looked at Daniel and asked, "Am I allowed to ask them questions?"

"Absolutely," he said, beaming like a proud papa.

I walked over to one of the seniors. He was wearing a baseball hat pulled down low over his face. I could tell that he had dark features even though most of his face was obscured with the hat and a full dark beard. He was thick and slightly taller than me. His chest was massive and covered with the same heavy dark fur that was on his face. His biceps were tremendous and I fantasized about them holding me down.

"Mind if I touch?" I asked him.

"Knock yourself out," he answered in a gruff tone that started the familiar tingle in my balls.

I placed my palm flat on his big hairy belly and felt the heat pouring off of his skin. Running my hand up his chest to his thick neck, I stepped behind him.

"What's your name, stud?" I asked in almost a whisper.

"Cal—" He choked. "Calvin."

I smiled at the effect I knew I was having on him. "Mind if I remove your hat, Calvin?"

"No."

I reached forward and grabbed the brim of his baseball hat and pulled it off of him. He had a closely shaved head which really turned me on. I put his hat back on, but backwards and stepped back in front of him. He looked totally hot and his dark eyes burned a hole in me.

Turning my eyes down to his crotch, I saw a pretty big out-line of a cock in his uniform pants. I grabbed it and found it to be hard as steel. "You are my first pick, stud!" I said loud enough for them all to hear.

Calvin blew a huge breath out of his mouth as if he had been holding it the whole time. "Thank you, Jesus."

"Thank *you*," I said, moving on.

I examined several other seniors before stepping through their line to the juniors. There was a very handsome junior with long blond hair and a tanned muscular body that looked like a surfer's. He had intrigued me at the pool party over the weekend and I was anxious to talk to him now. His eyes were locked onto mine the whole time I worked my way down his row. He was aggressive, unlike a lot of these guys. He knew he was the best-looking player in the room and he was anx-ious to get my attention.

"You think you can make the grade, surfer dude?" I asked him as I approached. The other players chuckled.

"Definitely."

"Why's that?" I questioned him.

"None of these other guys have this," he said, indicating his face and body. He put his hands behind his neck which outlined his biceps beautifully and then shimmied his whole body.

"And you think that is worthy of my attention?"

"You tell me," he challenged me.

"What's your name?" I asked, even though I already knew it.

"Hamilton," he said, grinning with beautiful white teeth.

I didn't like the cockiness so much, but I was loving his confidence. I also liked the way he moved. "Yeah, I think you might be worth my attention, Hamilton. You are my second pick."

"Fucking straight!" Hamilton yelled. His team mates all

laughed.

I stepped away from Hamilton and in front of the row of sophomores. I knew I was close to my shaggy freshman distraction, so I stepped through that row until I was face-to-face with him.

Shaggy was looking down again. I walked past him and then back to him. He was only slightly taller than me, but significantly wider. He was muscular, but not overly so. His chest was smooth except for a patch of hair at the base of his neck that expanded across the top of his chest. His nipples were so hard and small that all I wanted was to suck and bite them. Instead, I put a finger under his chin and lifted his eyes to mine. I could feel the bristle of his chin against my finger and something like electrical sparks flying between the two.

Shaggy's eyes reminded me of swirling golden sand. The flecks in them seemed to be in constant movement and I was drawn to him even more than before. He smelled like a real man and I couldn't get enough of breathing his scent into my nasal cavities.

"What's your name, fish?" I asked, using the derogatory term that the team used for freshmen and I heard them laugh at my use of it. I already knew his name, but I wasn't going to let the team know that I had researched them.

"Marcus," he said quietly.

"Good name," I said, letting go of his chin. He held my gaze for two seconds before his head bowed again. "Look at me," I demanded.

He looked back up, but this time I saw something different in his eyes. *He didn't like being ordered around? He didn't take direction well?* I didn't know what it was, but I did like a challenge.

"Do you think you are worthy of my attention, Marcus?"

He swallowed hard, with a big sharp-looking Adam's apple bobbing in his thick neck. "I want you, but there are others who are more worthy."

Perfect answer! "We'll see about that. You have potential and you are my third pick."

A gasp went up from the crowd at my unorthodox pick. I looked down the row of freshmen and saw that Jared had leaned forward to look at us. Narrowing my eyes, I pushed between the players until I was in front of them again. I was looking for the center and I found him near the end of the front line.

"Aren't you usually in the middle of the line?" I smirked to him once I was face to face with the big center. He was tall, at least six-six and heavy. His shirt and pants were off and he had a big thick tire around his waist. He was muscular with fat on top of it and tattooed with full sleeves. His chest and stomach were completely hairless. His head was shaven clean, but he had a patch of red hair on his chin.

The players laughed and the center asked, "You know football?"

"Of course."

"Isn't that unusual for you . . . marked guys?"

"Yeah, but I'm not your ordinary marked guy," I answered.

"I'll say." he smiled and grabbed his cock that was barely being contained by his sweaty jock.

"Do I make you hard, center?"

"Yes," he said before laughing.

"Good. What's your name?"

"Glen with one *n*."

"Nice to meet you, Glen with one n," I said as I grabbed his cock through the wet mesh of his jock strap. "You are my fourth pick!"

Glen let out a roar that echoed for a while in the small space. I moved back to the front and said to Daniel that I was done. I could see the look of disappointment on his face, but he accepted it with good humor.

"Well, boys, most of us didn't get picked this round, so we will have to wait and see what happens." The QB turned to me and asked, "What's next?"

"I've never had to plan out my fucking life with a team before," I said in disbelief.

"You have never been one of ours before. We will protect you, include you, and at least one of us will give you all the hard cock you want. And for those privileges you belong to us."

I sighed and said, "Well, I guess stud number one over there, Calvin, and I can grab something to eat tomorrow after his practice."

"Excellent. I will give each of your selections your cell number."

This was starting to feel more and more like some kind of cult—a huge throbbing mass of masculine meat cult, but a cult nonetheless. They were a little too involved and invested in me, but I was willing to play this little scenario out. The four men that I had picked to get to know better were certainly my type and my ass was itching to be fucked by all four of them as I left that locker room.

Maybe this cult wasn't so bad after all.

CHAPTER EIGHT

The word spread pretty quickly in my dorm that I had four dates with football players this week. The boys in my dorm, who had of course, never been on a date of any kind were fascinated by the subject and pumped me for details. When I refused to give them much, they just started a pool.

I came back from my afternoon classes on Tuesday and a lot of my dorm mates were hanging out on the wooden benches in the Quad right in front of our dorm. They had hung a poster showing the football team on the front door and were taking bets about whom the four players would be to take me out.

There were odds written by all of the names and I laughed out loud when I saw it.

"Good. I thought you might be offended," CJ, a junior from the third floor, said to me.

"Hell no! I think it is awesome and only wish that I could get in on it."

"Tell us how close we are, Loch!" someone yelled.

I approached the poster and saw that they were not very close. They had of course ranked the stars of the team very high, but they had done this from a sport fan perspective and not from my more personal perspective as a person who chose based on how much I would want to get fucked by these players.

All of the freshmen had very low odds, including Marcus. These odd makers weren't even factoring them into the equation at all. I smiled to myself, knowing that they were going to be really badly surprised.

"Looks like you did a very thorough job, boys," I told them. "Good luck!"

"What time is the first one happening?" someone asked.

"He's supposed to come over after practice ends at six."

"Awesome, we will order pizza and wait!"

Oh great. An audience. That shouldn't make it awkward or any-thing . . .

Most of the boys were drinking beer already and I feared that they would be totally soused by six, but it gave them something to do with their time. I had not showered that day, so I went upstairs to get ready.

My friends were waiting for me in Bob's room across the hall from mine. His door was open so that I could see they had gathered.

"Fellas, what's up?" I asked, standing in the doorway.

"Hey, Loch. You okay with what the guys are doing out front?"

"It's fucking hysterical, isn't it?"

Brandon looked relieved and said, "We didn't know what you would think about it."

"I think that those fucks don't have a clue as to whom I would choose, but you four do. I didn't see your names up on the betting sheet, so I suggest all four of you go down there and get into the action."

"They will think we had inside information," Dave pointed out.

"Do you?"

"No, you haven't said anything."

"Then go do it. I'm sure some of you will miss and they will know that you didn't know."

Jeremy asked, "You sure you don't mind, Loch?"

"Hell no! Go win some money while I get showered."

I went to my room, stripped, grabbed what I needed, and went to the common bathroom. I spent the next hour showering, shaving, and manscaping. I didn't think that Calvin would mind a little extra hair since he was a yeti himself, but I had nothing else to do but wait anyway, so I kept at it.

Within the hour, I was ready and went to lie down. I couldn't sleep of course, but the quiet time was awesome, even though I couldn't keep my mind from racing. There was a nice breeze blowing through the windows and I could clearly hear my dorm-mates waging their bets below me.

A little after six, I got a text from Calvin that he was on his way. I pulled on a pair of khaki cargo pants and an *Adidas* t-shirt and headed down to the bench outside.

The boys were a little drunker and a lot louder when I emerged. They cheered and slapped me on the back as I sat down on the end of the bench.

I saw Calvin emerge from the Pit seconds before the rest of the rowdy guys on the bench spotted him. He was in basketball shorts which showed off his muscular hairy legs and high-top sneakers. His hairy chest was hidden behind a UNC football t-shirt. What really did it for me was that he had his black baseball hat on and he was wearing it backwards, just like I wanted.

A yell brought me out of my head. "Holy shit! It's Calvin Thomas!"

The boys had spotted him and he was quickly closing the gap across the quad towards us. There were a lot of cheers that went up from the bench and a few groans. It seemed that the majority of the guys had picked him, so they were all ecstatic about the contest and about meeting Calvin.

He stopped right in front of me and smiled.

"I like the hat, stud." I smirked.

"Thought you might," he said, smiling broader and showing a beautiful set of teeth. He looked down the bench and asked, "What's this all about?"

"The boys have a little pool going on, guessing who the

four players are that I picked yesterday. Don't tell them." That was the last chance I got to talk to Calvin for a while as he was swamped by the sports-crazed NOMARs of my dorm. I watched as my dorm mates ran up to their rooms and got all kinds of paraphernalia for him to sign. They touched him and looked at him much as I did in that locker room yesterday, but for very different reasons.

Calvin eventually raised his voice and announced, "Boys, I need to go pay a little attention to this guy over here!" He inched towards me through the crowd. Much to my credit or their respect for Calvin as a sports God, the boys of my dorm parted like the Red Sea and he swiftly moved right up to me.

I was sitting at the back of the bench, so I was right at eye-level with the huge Calvin. He stopped right in front of my spread legs and put a heavy paw on each of my thighs and squeezed them.

"You ready to go, big guy?" he asked me, suddenly very serious.

I leaned in and put my lips beside his ear. "Feels good having you between my legs," I whispered. I knew that he would totally get turned on by my words and I needed to take him for a test drive, so I planned on getting him as hot and bothered as possible during dinner.

Calvin grabbed my hand and pulled me off the bench to a standing position. I guess that meant that we were ready to go. I waved goodbye to my buddies from the dorm and headed towards Franklin Street. Instead of taking the shortcut through the arboretum, Calvin led me up Raleigh Street. I figured that he just wasn't as familiar with Upper Campus like I was, so I let him go. Once on Franklin, we crossed and headed down a side residential street.

"Where are we going?" I asked.

Just then he stopped and opened a metal gate onto a sidewalk and held it open for me. The house was a Dutch colonial and in really good shape, but I didn't know these people from Adam, so I hesitated.

"It belongs to one of the boosters," Calvin explained. "He's only here for the games on the weekends and Coach said that we could use it to . . . entertain you this week."

"Wait, the coach knows about this little game?"

"Of course. It's all we talk about at practices and in the locker room."

We had slowly walked up to the door while he was explaining. I watched as Calvin pulled a key out of his shorts and started to unlock the door. "Aren't we going to go eat?" I asked, still a little thrown off by this house.

Calvin Thomas turned to me as he opened the door and said, "We can order a pizza in a minute, if you want to. I want to fuck you as soon as possible and as often as possible. Isn't that what you want?"

His bluntness made me smile and I didn't have the heart to tell him that there was more to this interview than fucking. But the answer to his question was obvious. I took on a more flirtatious stance and repeated his phrasing back to him, "Yes, I want you inside and on top of me as soon and as often as possible."

"Hot damn! Let's do this," he said, pushing me through the open door and closing it behind him. Calvin held onto my bicep with one big meaty hand as he pushed me in front of him towards a staircase. I heard a phone ringing and saw that he was calling someone on his cell phone with his other hand.

"Yes. Can I have two large pizzas and a two-liter of Coke delivered to one-fourteen Raleigh Street . . . cash . . . thanks." Calvin disconnected the call at the top of the stairs and directed me into a bedroom with a huge king-sized sleigh bed in it.

Finally letting go of my arm, Calvin said, "I have been waiting for this moment since you walked into that locker room yesterday. I can't believe that you picked me, especially over some of those other guys."

"Why wouldn't I pick you," I asked as I dropped my shorts and kicked my tennis shoes off.

He pulled his t-shirt off, revealing his hairy chest, and I nearly swooned. "Because of this," he said, indicating his hairy chest. "Most of the guys in the locker room make fun of me for it, but you seemed to like it."

Running my hand through his chest hair, I looked him directly in the eyes. "I not only like it, I love it," I told him. I quickly removed my socks, shirt, and boxer briefs.

"Wow," Calvin said.

"What?"

"Your ass. It's beautiful," he said with a husky voice as he ran his rough hand over my smooth skin, causing goose bumps to develop.

"What's beautiful is in here, stud," I chuckled as I dropped to my knees on the carpeted floors in front of Calvin and pointed at his crotch.

I pulled down his basketball shorts and his jock strap to reveal a beautiful piece of meat. Calvin's cock was about seven inches long and fat. He had a fat cock head that I immediately gorged myself on. He tasted like soap, probably from the locker room showers and he started to leak thick syrupy pre-cum as I sucked on him.

Calvin groaned as I swallowed his meat to its base. He had a lot of pubic hair, but it smelled clean so I didn't mind burying my face in it. He held my head there until I found it hard to breath and pulled back off of him.

"Goddamn!" Calvin groaned as I pistoned up and down on his big pole.

I smiled up at him, but he had his eyes closed so I pulled off of him and pushed his hard cock up onto his bristly stomach. This gave me total access to his big hairy balls, which I licked and sucked until they were soaking wet.

"You are incredible," Calvin said, breathing heavily.

I could tell that he was close to losing it, so I spit out his balls out and asked, "Want me to keep going or not?"

He answered by grabbing my head on both sides, face-fucking me with gusto. It took less than a minute for the huge linebacker to bust his nut and pour hot man-cream down my throat. I had assumed that because his body was so massive that his load would be also, but it was very manageable. Licking my lips, I cleaned his big dark-red shaft for him and noticed that he was sweating under his body sweater.

"Grrrrr!" he roared suddenly. Calvin reached down, grabbed me under the arms, and tossed me onto the bed.

This action didn't frighten me, because I could feel Calvin's lust pouring off of him in waves. In fact, I found it to be quite sexy—this aggressive animal side of him.

Calvin's cock was wet from my saliva, but I needed him to lube that big tool, so I stopped him with a firm arm to his furry stomach. He looked at me with confusion for a second and then he figured it out. He reached into the nightstand drawer and pulled out a bottle of lube. He squirted it on his palm and began to massage his still-swollen joint.

"Pour some here," I instructed him as I lifted my legs back onto myself and pointed at the top of my crack. He did and watched eagerly as it ran towards my rosebud. When the cold lube got there, I pushed it inside with one of my fingers and the flames practically consumed Calvin's dark eyes as his passion was turned to its highest setting.

Calvin held my legs down against my chest as he kneeled on the bed with one knee. Feeding his cock into my slickened hole, Calvin let out a low rumble from deep in his chest. His moan got louder the deeper he sank inside me.

"Fuck me! Your sweet hole is so fucking tight. Squeezing me so good . . ."

Suddenly the door bell rang, echoing in the almost empty house.

I felt bad for Calvin, who had just sunk to the nuts inside of my tight ass. I felt bad for myself, who was going to have him withdraw and I would be left with the world's worst feeling—the emptiness that comes after having your anal ring stretched out.

Still waiting for the inevitable uncoupling, I saw a wicked thought cross the large footballer's face and then a grin spread out over his bristly face.

CHAPTER NINE

Calvin Thomas had just speared me like a bear grabbing a fish in a stream, but before he could enjoy his reward, the doorbell had rung and halted his fuck.

"Put your hands around my neck," he commanded me.

What was he planning? I liked him ordering me around . . .

I locked my fingers behind his thick neck and he raised my legs onto his massive shoulders. I felt his hands slide under my back. Then, as if he was doing a squat in the weight room, Calvin lifted me up into the air while he stood up straight and then slightly arched backwards. I was still impaled on his throbbing prick, so I was held tight onto him, but I still didn't know what he was doing.

"Hold tight," he grumbled as he turned and headed out of the bedroom. When we arrived at the top of the stairs, I became frightened.

"Close your eyes, big guy. I got you," he said when he saw the look of fear on my face.

Calvin slowly negotiated the wide wooden stairs down to the front door. Arriving safely at the bottom, I opened my eyes with relief and felt him plant my back against the wall beside the front door. Looking up into his face, I saw him smirk as he thrust into me a couple of times as I was pinned against the wall.

This new position caused his body to be completely pressed against mine. His thick mat of fur pressed up against my cock which was becoming hard. Each thrust caused his hairy belly to rub the bottom of my shaft like a furry glove and I was harder than ever.

Suddenly, he opened the door, right as he drilled into my ass again. The stunned pizza guy was standing there, holding two large pies.

"Calvin Thomas," he muttered in disbelief.

"Yeah. Gimme those," Calvin said as he grabbed the pizza boxes.

The delivery guy looked at me and watched as Calvin thrust into me again. "Hey, can I get in on this action?" he asked as he grabbed his junk through his jeans as he set the 2-liter bottle down inside the door.

No fucking way! That pizza guy was a greasy stoner and I will completely walk if Calvin even suggests it.

"No way, man," Calvin laughed, to my relief. "This sweet ass is all mine." The pizza delivery guy looked disappointed. "Charge it to the football department like usual. They will give you a big tip."

"I think I am getting the big tip right now!" I said breathlessly.

Both of the guys laughed and the delivery guy left. Calvin continued to thrust into me while I was planted on that wall.

"You—are—the—fucking—real—deal," Calvin moaned, accentuating each word with a hard thrust.

It was at that point that I knew he was going to keep us pinned there until his release. I was on the edge myself from the constant friction of Calvin's hairy belly against my hard cock.

"I'm going to come," I moaned into his neck.

Calvin grunted, "Let me come first."

I didn't know if that was possible, but I tried. Calvin came in a hard thrust, a huge grunt, and a hot shot of cum into my bowels. I didn't wait any longer. My piss hole opened up and I shot a big load of hot sticky cum into his thick chest hair. My body shuddered with my climax and I started to slide down the wall from the sweat building up on my back.

We wound up in a huddled mass on the floor. Calvin knew how to fuck and proceeded to put on quite a show of it. He screwed me four more times that night and afterwards, I was left wondering if I would be able to walk back home in the morning.

Calvin fell asleep on the bed finally while I gingerly walked to the big bath tub I had seen in their master bath. Soaking for a few hours sounded like a fantastic idea.

An hour or four more infusions of hot water later, Calvin appeared at the door. He was completely dressed.

"I'm going to go," he said with a shrug of his shoulders.

"Okay," I answered, stunned by the fact that he was leaving. *He wasn't even going to wait around to walk me home?*

"I had a really great time."

"Thanks. Me, too."

"I'm gone!" he said, as he turned to leave. I looked down and then back up when I heard him turn around. "I hope that you will want to do that again . . . you know, like . . . everyday . . . for the rest of the year."

I could see the raw emotion on his dark visage under the brim of his hat, despite his lack of manners. Surprised by how much this meant to him, I nodded so I wouldn't have to answer. He told me to lock the door when I left and then he was gone.

However, I already knew my decision about Calvin Thomas. He was a great fuck, but not very considerate of me. He had shown it in several different ways throughout the night, but most importantly I did not feel that he was the one for me. He was exciting sexually, but not the type of sex that could withstand more than a few weeks.

I knew that my next date, with Hamilton, the surfer dude, wasn't until Thursday night, so I had some time to rest up. I spent the night in the spare bedroom of the football booster's house, since there were multiple wet spots on the master bed's sheets. I did not want to walk home alone in the dark, so I thought this was for the best. Taking another hot bath in the morning, I was able to sneak back into my dorm undetected to change clothes for my first class.

Class was uneventful, but my boys were waiting for me when I came home after the last one.

"We were worried when you didn't come home from dinner," Dave said when he saw me.

"Not like we were watching for you or anything . . ." Jeremy added sheepishly.

I looked at their well-intentioned faces and reassured them, "Well, if you would have been, I would have appreciated it."

"How was it?" Brandon pried.

"It was good."

"But?" Bob asked.

I laughed at how well they knew me over such a short period of time. "But, he's not for me."

"He didn't hurt you, did he?" Dave asked in horror.

"No, no, he was fine. Just not right for me to . . . see on a regular basis," I said with a sigh. "I'm so lucky to have you guys watching over me, but I gotta crash, fellas."

The boys started moving towards the door. I told them that I would like to go to dinner tonight if they wanted to, before I shut and locked the door. I pulled down the blinds and fell asleep immediately.

Later that night at dinner I didn't give the boys too many details, but I did tell them about the booster's house and how nice it was. They asked where Calvin took me to dinner and I had to admit that he had not. They were just as astonished as I was that night.

My ass was just starting to feel right again by the time Thursday afternoon rolled around. I repeated my cleaning regime and joined my dorm brothers on the bench outside to wait for my date. I didn't think many of them would be surprised that I had picked Hamilton Joyce with my second selection.

I was caught off guard when shortly after six, a black truck pulled into the parking lot beside the quad and beeped the horn. We all looked over and I saw the center, Glen Capshaw, waving at me. Glen had been my *third* pick, not my second, so I got up and walked over to the driver's side window of the truck.

"Expecting to see that fake pretty-boy surfer?" he asked me with a huge fucking grin.

"Yeah, I was," I said quickly.

"He's a junior. The seniors go first. Hop in. Hamilton was pretty disappointed when I told him," Glen said, starting to chuckle.

By now, the boys on the bench had figured out that this was my second date and were surrounding the truck to meet him. They all knew him, of course, and were ready with things for him to sign. From what I could hear, most of them had not picked him based on his larger size.

Letting the crowd die down, I finally slipped into the passenger seat and waved bye to my buddies.

"Where you wanna eat?" Glen asked as he pulled up to turn around in the cramped parking area.

Surprised that Calvin had not told him to just go and fuck me, I answered, "Anywhere you want, would be fine by me."

"If we go to Top of the Hill, we can eat for free," he informed me.

"Sounds like a plan," I said with a grin.

"It's owned by a former player and they never charge us when we eat there."

"That's pretty awesome." That must have cost the owner a fortune. I could only imagine how much those big boys could eat.

"Sure is."

We found a spot to park on the street and didn't even have to wait for a table. I was discovering that these football players led a charmed life, at least in this community. I had also figured out that if the players were going to go in order of age for my dates, that I wasn't going to get to see shaggy Marcus until much later in the week than I had planned. Not having realized that I was looking forward to it as much as I was, I recognized my disappointment.

After ordering, Glen looked at me and said, "So, you looking forward to tonight?"

"What's tonight?"

He cocked his head to the side and answered, "We're going to the house that you and Calvin went to."

"Oh, yeah. Sorry, I thought you meant something else." I felt stupid again in front of the big lineman, but at least I was getting a good meal out of this date.

Glen laughed and said, "Calvin told us in the locker room that you were amazing."

"Really?"

"Yeah, he couldn't stop talking about you, and the guys were worked up into a frenzy by the time practice started."

I wasn't happy that Calvin had kissed and told. "What else did he say?" I asked as our salads arrived.

"He said that after the fucking he gave you that night, the other three of us might as well not even go out with you."

"Did he?" I asked with a smirk. "But, you did anyway."

"Fuck, yes! He can suck my cock if he thinks I'm not going to—" He stopped when he realized what path he was heading down.

"Get your cock sucked?" I finished for him as the waiter brought our entrees.

He smiled sideways and said, "Yeah. Is that wrong?"

"Not really. I just wished I wasn't a done deal."

"You still have the power to say no, but I think because you picked the four of us as your favorites, that it is kinda a done deal," Glen admitted.

"I guess. So, that's what you want to do, Glen with one *n*?"

"Hell yeah. I mean, if you want to also."

"Then let's get out of here," I said as I put my fork down on my plate.

Glen grinned like a fool and took care of the check for us by handing it to the manager. He drove his truck to the same booster's house that I had been in with Calvin. I was pleased to see that someone had come in and cleaned up since then.

Glen stripped and then lay down on the fresh sheets on his back. Even though Glen had a day's worth of scruff on his face, his hefty body was smooth as a baby's bottom. His big round belly fascinated me, but his long hooked cock really held my attention. He held it up for me and I wondered if it was because he couldn't see it past his belly.

"You want me to make a long snap from center?" I smirked at him as I removed the rest of my clothes.

Glen shook his big head and grinned. "It is such a huge fucking turn-on to have you say things like that."

"I aim to please." I climbed up onto the bed with him. Kneeling beside his crotch, I sucked his long member into my hot mouth and gave him a good vacuuming.

And that was pretty much how the rest of the night went for us. Glen never moved off of that bed or his back. He had just enough energy to drop a huge load of hot man-cream in my mouth and then let me suck him back up hard. I rode his long prick until he busted his nut deep inside of me and then he fell asleep. The next morning, I blew him again and then rode him to his climax.

It did nothing for me except make my legs sore. Glen just didn't have enough energy to be with me on a regular basis and I was glad that I was finding out now and not after I had picked him. He was a nice guy and I was glad that I got to know him better, but he was not the man for me, either.

CHAPTER TEN

Hamilton Birch was a unique man. The surfer look-a-like arrived in the quad on Saturday morning on a Harley. I had to give it to him, it was quite the entrance. The boys from my dorm also gave him quite the ovation. Most of them had picked him in the pool and couldn't wait to meet him.

The footballer got off his bike and high-fived most of the guys on the bench. Hamilton winked at me and handed me his helmet as he worked the crowd. His long blond hair swirled around him as he constantly pulled it back behind his ears. Hamilton might be the best-looking guy that I had ever been with.

I rode on the back of his bike as he drove to Jordan Lake. It was a little thrilling to spoon onto his broad back and hold him around the waist as he drove. I took the time to grab his hard cock through his jeans as we were riding. He was long and thick and felt hard as steel.

He yelled back to me, "You're going to be riding on that in a couple minutes, baby. Be patient."

I didn't stop playing with him and by the time we reached the lake, the front of Hamilton's jeans was wet. He was leaking a tremendous amount of pre-cum and my cock hardened as I played with him. He parked the bike and it looked as though we were alone on this side of the lake.

Hamilton immediately stripped off his clothes, saying, "I love the sun on my naked body, don't you?"

I couldn't say that I've ever felt it before, but I nodded to him as I stripped off my clothes. I guess I wasn't going to get dinner, but looking at Hamilton's hard body and thick cock, made me not want food so much. He was absolutely beautiful and knew it.

"You hungry, baby?" he asked me.

"I could wait," I answered with a smirk.

"I'm going to feed you my steak then." He smirked back.

"Yum! My favorite." I carefully dropped to my knees in the rocky sand as Hamilton approached me. His cock was already sticking out from his crotch and the pre-cum was glistening on the head like dew on a blade of grass.

"I got what you need, baby." Hamilton moaned loudly as he pushed his hard cock into my mouth.

I swiped his piss hole with my tongue as he pushed it inside my hungry hole and got a big dollop of man-honey for a reward. Savoring his nectar, I swallowed it and then turned my full attention to licking and sucking him. He truly was blessed with a great wiener to go along with the face and body.

I sucked on Hamilton's prick with long pulling draws. He continued to leak a lot of pre-cum and I continued to capture every drop just like he was a melting Freeze Pop. The surfer-turned football player reached down and grabbed both sides of my head and turned my face up to his.

"I wanna blow my load all over your pretty face, baby."

"Yes, sir," I said, just because I knew it would inflame him even more. This man was so exciting and I liked everything about him. *Could he be the one? Quite possibly.*

"Oh, baby," he moaned, pulling his hard cock out of my mouth and stroking it right in front of my face. It only took a few strokes up and down the long shaft before Hamilton blew his load. I closed my eyes and opened my mouth as I felt the hot cream hit my face.

He came a lot, and all of it landed on my upturned face or in my mouth. Shocked that his man-cream was so bitter, I immediately wondered what he had eaten to cause this chemical reaction. *Asparagus, Brussel sprouts, some kind of weird cheese? Maybe this was what he always tasted like. If that was the case, this was going to be a deal breaker.*

Hamilton, much to my chagrin, used his large cock head as a paint brush and wiped the cum on my face into my mouth. The bitter cum burned my throat as he fed me, but I swallowed anyway.

"That was amazing, baby," Hamilton cooed over me as he lifted me up off of my knees.

He kept one hand around my biceps and guided me towards a fairly new pier that had been built out over the water. Walking me out onto the pier, Hamilton directed me to the furthest point out onto the water.

"I want to fuck you right here, baby," he said, his voice husky with his need.

I looked around in each direction. "Right here?"

He smiled and said, "Right here."

"What if someone comes and sees?"

"They will be jealous as hell!" He dismissed my concerns with a large grin.

The boards of the pier had recently been replaced and looked smooth enough, but I knew they would hurt as Hamilton pounded me into them. I had to manipulate this situation in order to gain the most pleasure for me.

"Lie down," I ordered him, waiting to see how he would take to it. Hamilton smiled easily and lowered himself down onto the planks.

"Spread your legs." Hamilton, like every NOMAR I had ever met, could not stay in the dominating role very long. I could always manipulate myself into the domineering role whenever I felt it necessary. It was a little bit of a let-down, but I didn't know any difference.

He did. I knelt between his legs and I sucked on his dick that still had some cum in it from the facial he just gave me.

He got hard in seconds, which was a huge plus in my book. I needed a lot of saliva on his thick monster since neither one of us seemed to have any lube. Once he was totally wet, I spit into my hand and put my saliva on the ends of two fingers, which I then slipped onto and into my asshole.

Straddling Hamilton, I went down to my knees on either side of his stomach and lowered my ass onto his throbbing cock. He helped by holding his thick joint at the base for me.

Hamilton's wide cock head pressed against my puckered hole until it popped inside. My anal ring stretched wide to accommodate his girth and squeezed his meat missile tightly as I slid down onto him. Throwing my head back and squeezing my eyes shut, I groaned loudly as I impaled myself on him.

"That's it, baby. Take all of that big dick," he urged me.

With his words inflaming me, I continued to push until I was sitting on his crotch and his entire massive joint was inside of me. Hamilton ran his hands up my side as I got used to his large member splitting me in half.

God, this could be the one. I enjoyed the feeling of Hamilton filling me up. I could have this every day for two years.

Hamilton slowly brought me out of my thoughts by starting to move his lower half up and down underneath me. He was soon pulling his thick cock out of me and then thrusting back inside me as I leaned forward over his muscled chest. I braced my arms on his well-defined pecs and enjoyed the view.

After Glen's passive fucking two days ago, I was grateful that Hamilton was willing to work for my ass. He started to fuck me harder and deeper as he reached another climax.

"Get up!" Hamilton said, smacking me on the ass with a flat hand.

Shocked by his command, I looked into his eyes and saw that he wasn't kidding. "I want you to eat my load, baby," he moaned.

Really? I have to taste that nasty shit again? Maybe it won't be so bad this time.

But, yes, it was. Hamilton's cum was just as bitter and strong as it was the first time, but I swallowed and smiled as he milked every last drop into my hot mouth. I used the old porn star trick of spitting his cum back onto his cock as I attempted to clean him and then let it fall off of him.

I continued to blow him until he was ready to go again. "Sit on the side of the pier with your legs hanging over," I ordered.

Watching him follow my command, I knew that Hamilton was not the man for me. Not because his cum tasted bitter, or that he had the penchant for wanting that cum to always be on my face or in my mouth, but because he was perfectly fine with letting me command him.

"Like this?" he asked, his face full of childish excitement while he flashed a brilliantly white set of teeth.

"Like that!" I laughed at him. Starting to walk towards him, I heard a sound behind me and quickly turned to see what it was. I was shocked to see two students emerging from the bushes. They were intently watching Hamilton and me.

"We have company," I said to Hamilton without turning to look at him.

"They just want a little show," he said in a voice that let me know that he had known they were there long before I did. "Let's give it to them."

"You sure?" I had no desire for this to get out of hand. The fact that he was risky with my safety also told me that he was not the right man for me.

"Sure," Hamilton reassured me as he helped lower me into his lap and held me tight to his broad chest as I pushed his cock back into my hole. "I love being in there, baby."

Hamilton had some exhibitionist in him, and that was definitely not something I was interested in, but I let him fuck me right there on the end of the pier in front of a gathering crowd of students, some of whom openly jacked their dicks while watching.

Afterwards, Hamilton and I stopped to have bar-b-que sandwiches before he dropped me off at my dorm. He told me that he had enjoyed himself, but was so confident that I would pick him to be with for the next two years, that he didn't even ask me to consider it.

CHAPTER ELEVEN

Marcus Battle was my last date and the one that I had been looking forward to the most. He was my age and not nearly as sexy as the other three football players that I had been out with, but there was something about him that drew me to him.

After doing my routine primping for him, I went downstairs and eyed the dorm's pool chart. My friend, Dave, was in first place and I saw that no one had picked Marcus to get selected by me for a possible boyfriend. I knew that meant that Dave had won the pool and I smiled to myself as I turned from it.

I felt Marcus before I saw him. He was walking across the quad towards me and my body began ringing like a bell. His shaggy dirty blond hair was dangling in front of his face as his head was lowered. Normally there was a lot of hooting and hollering about now, but this time I looked over at my friends from the dorm and saw that they had no clue who this was walking towards them.

Marcus walked right up to me and said, "Hi."

"Hey, Marcus," I replied.

A guy from the fourth floor named Ed was watching us and then asked, "Wait, this isn't the guy, is it?"

"It is," I answered. "Sorry that none of you guys picked him in your pool."

"Who is it?" someone else asked.

I smiled at Marcus and introduced him to the crowd, "This is Marcus War. He's a freshman from Ohio. He plays tight end."

Some of the guys shook his hand and others grumbled when they realized that they had not won the pool and dispersed. Marcus and I were soon mostly alone.

"Wanna grab something to eat?" Marcus asked me. His voice was deep and seemed to vibrate through me like an echo. "And then you can explain what this is all about."

"Yeah. I'm craving Time Out for chicken and biscuits. That okay with you?"

"That's good. Coach says I have to put on some weight anyway." We started walking towards Franklin Street. I remembered that he was just a little bit taller than I was, just as I noticed how broad he was. His aura made him seem so much bigger.

I caught Marcus watching me as we walked. He didn't seem as cowed and unsure of himself as the other times that I had seen him, but then again, I didn't know him really well. I remembered when he told me with the look in his eyes that he didn't like taking my commands in the locker room and I was once again totally intrigued by him.

We ordered dinner and took a seat while we waited. Marcus stared at me—I locked my green eyes onto his golden eyes. When he spoke, his words were well considered. "I was surprised that you picked me last week."

"Oh, yeah?" I asked, letting him sway in the wind for a bit.

"You created quite a stir." I couldn't help but smile. When I didn't respond, he continued, "The guys all look at me differently now just because you did that."

Raising an eyebrow, I asked, "Different better or different worse?"

"Different better," he said, grinning. His mouth was just a little on the small side and I noticed that when he showed his set of perfect white teeth, his squared chin jutted forward slightly. "They think I'm some kind of stud now and have been giving me shit all week about it."

"That's cool." I replied. "I'm glad that they see in you what I do."

The worker at the bar called our number. Marcus got up and delivered the food to the table.

"I can get the drinks," I offered quickly.

"I got it," he said in his low voice that made me tingle all over.

"Diet Coke, please." I watched him go to the drink fountain and noticed his strong thighs in his jeans. Marcus was already doing more for me than all the other guys had and was treating me like an equal at the same time.

We ate while we talked. He asked about my life and I asked about his. I liked that he was down-to-Earth and that he came from a small town outside the big city like I had. Marcus was smart and easy to talk to. After I finished eating, I was even more drawn to him than I had been before.

"Shall we go?" I asked as he finished the last bite of his chicken breast.

"Sure." Marcus grinned easily. That familiar burn started in my nut sack that signaled that I was about to have a very good time.

Without even saying anything to each other, we started to walk towards that house that the football booster was letting the team use. Marcus told me about his day including how practice went. He said that the guys had been a lot more aggressive to him since I had picked him.

"Sorry," I said, feeling guilty.

"Not a problem," he said smoothly. "I just tell them to bring the pain and they see that I'm ready."

I liked his confidence and was pleasantly surprised by it. In my other times I had been around him, I had not seen it. Entering the gate, Marcus let me lead the way up to the door.

"You want to do the honors, since you have been here

before?" he asked with a raised eyebrow.

I snatched the set of keys from his proffered hand. "Even though you NOMARs don't believe it, I like to put the key in the hole sometimes." I was thrilled to be sparring with him verbally and an itch deep inside my ass reminded me that we would be sparring physically soon.

"That's not going to happen here!" Marcus snorted as he snatched the keys back from me and opened the door. He headed to the side of the staircase and into the back of the house.

"Marcus, the bedrooms are upstairs," I called to him.

"We're not going to the bedroom," he called back without even turning around or stopping.

What? I followed behind him. He stopped in the living room which contained several wide leather sofas and a very large flat-screened TV.

"I thought we could watch some TV, if you wanted to." Marcus hung his head slightly and looked at me through his long bangs.

"I thought we were going to fuck," I said flatly.

"Who told you that?" he snapped, but flashed me a grin to soften the blow.

"I just assumed . . ."

"That's not happening," he said with finality.

"Why?" I asked in shock.

He looked into my eyes again and tilted his head slightly. "Didn't you get enough cock this week?"

It was like a slap in my face, but he was right and something about him made me want to tell him the truth. "I did," I admitted with a shrug.

"Yet, you still want more?"

"I want you," I said in self-defense.

"Not tonight," he said softly and grinned even more.

This man was more complex than even I gave him credit

for being. I was so disappointed that I wasn't going to get fucked by him tonight, but at the same time, I was thrilled that he had the will power to not do it, as well as intriguing me with his thought process. I caught myself staring at him with my mouth open.

"But we can watch TV together, if you want," Marcus repeated, raising his hand towards the flat-screen.

"Can I at least see your cock?" I asked, ignoring his statement again.

"No."

I couldn't keep the disappointment off my face or out of my voice. "But, how will I be able to tell if you are the one, if I don't at least see it?"

"Maybe you won't be able to . . ." He smirked.

Oh, is this the game we are playing? Bring it, shaggy! I had to admit to myself that I was super turned-on by the fact that Marcus was able to keep me on my toes. I had never met anyone who had the will power to turn down my sexual advances and it was quite attractive.

I put on a new face and said, "I guess we could watch some TV . . ."

"That'a boy," Marcus snorted. He led the way around one of the sofas which was in an L shape. He kicked off his *Adidas* tennis shoes and sat down in the corner with his legs up on the long side of the couch. His feet, clad in black athletic socks, were a lot bigger than I had realized. They were wide and long—making my cock hard as a rock.

I moved to sit down on the other end of the couch and Marcus immediately said, "Come sit with me, Loch."

What does he mean? I moved around the coffee table and hesitated, not knowing where to sit.

"Kick your shoes off," Marcus commanded.

I did.

"I would like you to sit here," he said as he indicated the

space between his outstretched legs. "Are you okay with that?"

I looked into his eyes, which held a playful expression. Was this going to happen? He was definitely flirting with me. I could feel the pull between us just as if he had tied a rope around my waist.

"I don't mind," I said with a gulp.

Marcus held up his arms and moved his fingers towards him in the international sign for *come here*. I turned around and lowered my ass to the couch while he pulled a thick leg up to make space for me. Once I was seated, he rested his sock-covered foot against my bare thigh. The smell of his foot beside me was intoxicating — the fresh soap smell of his skin combined with the musky sweat of his foot.

Looking over my shoulder at him, I watched as his small lips curled up on the ends. I looked back down at his foot and then impulsively, reached for it. Lifting it up, I pulled his foot into my lap and then slowly removed his sock.

I was hopeful that his feet would be as attractive to me as the rest of his body and it did not disappoint. The skin was slightly paler than the rest of his skin, and his toes were large and square. It was a powerful, masculine foot on a boy's body.

Sneaking a quick look at Marcus reclining into the couch cushions, I saw that he was curious about what I was going to do and smirking at me at the same time. I lay my hand on the top of his foot and heard his sharp intake of breath. An electric surge went through my hand as I made contact with him and felt the heat roll off of his foot. Taking his foot into my hands, I slowly started to rub and knead his powerful hoof.

"Fuck me," Marcus groaned in a deep guttural voice as I worked over his instep and heel.

"That's my plan," I said, starting to laugh. Moving to the bottom of his foot, I dug the heel of my palm into his sore muscles and kneaded them. I twisted and bent his foot, hearing the bones crack and pop in my hands as I manipulated them.

"Not tonight, Loch, not tonight," he said, shaking his shaggy head.

"All right," I said, purposely dragging it out to show my annoyance.

"But if it is anything like this foot rub, it will not be long." He groaned.

I finished his left foot and pulled his right foot from behind my back and onto my lap. Pulling his sock off, I was again overwhelmed with the smell of him and the heat of his closeness. I gave this foot the same treatment as the first one and smiled to myself as the big man moaned beside me.

As I finished rubbing Marcus' big dogs, it occurred to me that this was the most boyfriend-ish kind of thing I had ever done. He had only known me for about an hour or so, but he had already touched me in a way that my past boyfriends hadn't being able to accomplish in a year's time.

To reward him for those warm feelings he was giving me, I wanted to give him something pleasurable. I leaned forward to plant my lips on his big dogs and was stopped by a firm growl from Marcus. Surprised, I looked up at him quickly and saw his stern look. I grinned and kept moving towards his feet, now with my tongue out.

"Don't!" he said firmly.

When I acted like I was going to lick his feet anyway, Marcus grabbed me by the scruff of my neck with a giant hand that sent electric fingers of sexual current running right down my spine.

"Get up here where I can keep hold of you."

He directed me towards him with his hand as he lifted one leg around me. I slid right between his legs and onto his chest. My head and shoulders were resting on his broad chest and once I settled into place, he draped a big arm down the middle of my chest to hold me.

It was an incredibly intimate position and I could feel his rock-hard cock stabbing me in my lower back. I had never met anyone who was so commanding in private and so humble in public.

Marcus' voice was husky as hell when he spoke next. "I guess I have to hold you in place to keep you from doing things I don't want you to do . . ."

"I guess I'm not very good at following directions," I said sarcastically.

"You'll get better," he said immediately, as if he had thought about it before.

I was feeling something that I had never felt before. Never had I met a man who was able to resist my . . . *charms*, and he also was showing command over me. It was oddly disturbing and extremely exciting. My cock was so hard that it was painful.

I took the chance to study his hands. They, like his feet, were very masculine and square. His fingers were long and thick. The backs of his hands were covered lightly in copper-colored hair and bulging veins. Definitely hands that I wanted wrapped around me.

Marcus tapped me on the chest with his fingertips and said, "I heard what those boys said about you in the locker room."

Misunderstanding his intent for telling me this, I asked, "Did you like it?"

"No. I didn't like it at all." He was quiet and I wondered what they had said to give him such a strong reaction. When I didn't answer, he continued, "I don't think they treated you very well."

"Which part?"

"Loch, you are a person that is entitled to great respect and I didn't like that two of them just used you for their own pleasure."

"Some of it was my pleasure also," I admitted to him. As much as I was enjoying being this close and lying on top of him, it didn't allow me to look into his face and eyes to see how he was feeling.

"Well, I certainly know that, Loch. What you are doing for one of us is an incredible thing and I just think they should have been more appreciative of that."

"Oh, I think they were appreciative," I said, starting to chuckle.

"You know what I mean. They should have treated you like you were a person and not a piece of meat."

"Speaking of pieces of meat . . ."

"No!" Marcus laughed and put his other arm over my shoulders and onto my chest. "I will pin you down if I have to," he threatened me as he snaked his feet on top of my thighs and between my legs.

"Could be fun," I admitted.

"Will be fun," he corrected.

We watched an episode of *Elementary* and then Marcus walked me home. He had let me watch the whole show while lying on his chest, didn't fuck me, didn't let me blow him, and didn't let me see his cock. I had never been more satisfied in my life.

Chapter Twelve

M arcus had walked me home after the show was over. He absolutely had more will power than any NOMAR I had ever met. We stopped to say goodbye at the bench.

"I hope we can hang out again," Marcus said with a note of lust to his voice that he had been unable to control.

"I would like that."

"How about Friday after practice. I can come get you again."

"Awesome," I gushed, unable to bottle my excitement. I was already picturing him fucking me on Friday.

"Cool. I will wait here until you are safely in your room. Text me."

"Yes, sir!" I said, jagging him. "You sure you don't want to come up for a little while?"

"It wouldn't be for a little while, Loch."

I giggled at how his words and his smoldering stare combined to totally throw me off my game. "Yeah," I agreed.

"Goodnight."

"See ya." I unlocked the dorm door and headed upstairs. Once inside my room with the door locked, I texted him.

Safe!
Have a great night, Loch.
I'm not going to do anything but think of you . . .
Nothing else?
Haha! Yes, I will be jacking off thinking of you.
Awesome! See you Friday.

See you then, Marcus.

I didn't seem to sleep at all that night. There was something powerful that was happening inside me and I couldn't yet understand it. Marcus was in my head and had infected my body as well.

I was still tired when I got up for class the next morning. Daniel Lodge texted me during my third class of the day and wanted to know who I was picking. I told him that I wasn't quite ready to pick yet. He informed me that I would need to come by after practice to select some more candidates. I tried to say that I could do it myself, but he insisted.

After class, I called Marcus and told him about my text string with his quarterback.

"Hello?"

"Hey Marcus, its Loch."

"What's up?"

"Lodge texted me while I was in class and wanted to know who I was picking."

His voice was wary when he answered, "Okay."

"When I told him that I wasn't quite ready to make a pick yet, he insisted that I come to practice today and pick more guys to go out with."

There was a heavy sigh from the other side of the phone connection. "I thought that might happen."

"What should I do?"

"You'll have to pick one of us or you'll have to choose more guys to go out with. They will not allow anything else, I'm afraid."

"I don't really want to go out with more guys," I said softly.

"But you don't know enough to pick?" he asked with equal softness.

I hesitated, not knowing how to answer. "I think I do, but I want to be sure."

"Then you have to pick more guys to go out with," Marcus said resolutely and firmly.

"Okay," I said with resignation.

"I guess I will see you after practice today. That's a bonus for me."

"Yeah. See you then," I said, right before I disconnected the line. I was a little perturbed that he didn't give me more direction or tell me what he wanted me to do, even though I knew what that was. *Why did he have to be so goddamn respectful?*

I took off for Kenan Stadium at a quarter till six, so I would be there for the end of practice. When I wound my way down towards the locker room, I got a strange feeling. I slowed my pace and tried to identify what was different — it was the smell.

Entering the locker room, it smelled clean, like soap and deodorant. I saw that most of the players had showered and were getting dressed in their everyday clothes. A few stragglers were coming out of the showers either fully naked or with small white towels covering them. It was a sight to behold and the view made me lightheaded.

"Loch!"

Turning towards the voice which had called my name, I came face to face with Calvin. He was wearing cargo shorts, but nothing else. His hairy chest still glistened with small drops of water from the shower.

"Calvin," I greeted him with a grin.

"Hey. I'm glad that you are here. We're going to eat dinner first and then you can address the team."

"Cool." I got the distinct impression that Calvin was still one hundred percent sure that I was going to pick him to be my boyfriend. I hated to break his heart, but it had to be done. This experience was not going to be easy or enjoyable.

I nodded to Hamilton as he looked out from behind a set of lockers. I was looking for Marcus, hoping to see his naked body, when I felt a hand wrap around my arm and pull me. Turning, I saw that it was Glen and he was pulling me out of the locker room.

"C'mon baby. We're gonna go eat and then maybe you and me can find a dark corner in the equipment room to go have dessert in." His voice was laced with lust and need.

"Glen with one *n*, you are as subtle as ever," I said, verbally jabbing him.

"What's the point in beating around the bush?" His smile was infectious and made me chuckle. "My cock has already dumped a load of my seed inside of you. There are no games left that we need to play."

I conceded by saying, "I guess you're right."

"That's what I thought," he said triumphantly. Glen led me to a banquet hall where there was a buffet set up.

"This is the seniors' table. This is where you will sit," he said firmly while pointing at a table near the food. "I'm going to go take a piss and then we'll eat."

I had no plans to eat with Glen, so I went to get a drink and then stood around the sweet tea pitcher, waiting to see Marcus. He came in about a minute later, looking hot as hell in a pair of camo shorts, Army t-shirt, and flip-flops. His gaze locked on mine right away like I had a freaking homing device on me.

Marcus changed course and headed right for me. He stopped in front of me, his eyes blazing.

"Hey, Marcus," I managed to say before Calvin appeared.

Calvin put a big arm around Marcus' shoulders. "You know, this fish here has surprised us all. First, with him being picked in the contest and then he refused to give details about your date in the locker room." Calvin's tone was one of a school yard bully and I didn't care for it.

I watched as Marcus bowed his shaggy head and didn't say a word. The fact that he had refused to give details in the locker room made me like him even more.

"So, what's your secret, fish?" Calvin continued. He looked at me and asked, "Did he fuck you, Loch, or couldn't he get it up for that?"

"Calvin," I said sternly.

"Okay, okay," he said as he took his arm back. He looked around and saw that a little crowd had gathered around us. Calvin raised his voice so everyone could hear. "I know there is no way he fucked you like I did. You like it hard, deep, and dirty." The crowd laughed. "As well as, five or six times a night," Calvin added.

Again, the crowd laughed.

"Shut your fucking mouth, Thomas," Marcus said, without even raising his head. His voice was loud and firm and carried such a threat of violence that Calvin paused.

"Or what, fish?"

"Or you will ruin your chances with Loch," Marcus replied.

I gasped. I had expected him to say something about fighting, but now I saw that Marcus was smarter than that. He was appealing to the only thing that Calvin had no control over — my pick. *Smart, very smart.*

Calvin looked at me and I nodded my head. "Don't be a crude ass, Calvin. Nobody likes that."

"Sorry," Calvin said and stood in place, probably not knowing what to do next.

"I'm hungry," I announced. "It smells good."

"We'll get you a plate," a tall thick guy with a light brown beard said. He indicated his friend who was skinny with a heavy dark brown beard.

"Thanks," I said as I watched the crowd disperse.

Marcus turned with me and said quickly, "You have to sit with them. There is a hierarchy."

"But I want to sit with you."

"Not today, Loch," he said with finality as he walked away from me to a far table.

Hamilton was waiting there to escort me to his table, but Calvin stopped him with a smooth body block. The burly lineman escorted me to the seniors' table and forced me to sit between him and Daniel Lodge. Glen sat across from me and the two bearded players came with a big plate of food for me. They sat down beside Glen.

"Good lord," I said when I saw the amount of food on my plate.

"We didn't know what you liked, so we got you some of everything," the skinny one said.

"Thank you guys. I'm Loch."

"Like we don't know that," the bigger one said, rolling his eyes. "I'm Pushman and this is Smida."

"They are inseparable knuckleheads," Calvin said, snorting. "Laurel and Hardy."

"They are pretty different from each other," I said, smiling at them. They beamed at me.

Dinner was awkward, at best, with most of the seniors trying to get my attention and Glen and Calvin trying to block them out as best they could. I watched Marcus from across the room and saw him much the way I had that very first time I had seen him at the concert — interacting with his friends and being very carefree.

I picked at my dinner, but ate enough to be full. When most of the guys were finished, the quarterback stood up and got their attention.

"So boys, we are happy to have our marked friend Loch back with us tonight. He has been out with four of our teammates, so we are eager for his decision. Loch."

I didn't want to have to do this in front of all of them. Standing up slowly, I looked around the room. Marcus was staring right at me and his strong presence was helpful to me. *I can do this.*

I purposely chose to look at a section of the team that did not contain Calvin, Glen, Hamilton, or Marcus. I couldn't bear to see their faces of disappointment. "Sorry, boys, but I am unable to make a decision today."

The boys groaned and then cheered as they realized what it meant.

I continued when their vocalizations had died down. "My dates with your four representatives were awesome, but my last one with the freshman was interrupted, so I would like to go out with him again, so that I can get . . . to know him." I paused for comic effect and my arrow hit its mark as the crowd roared.

"So that's why he wouldn't give us any details," Calvin said to the table.

Daniel stood up beside me and said, "That's fine. You can go out with War again, but you will also have to pick three more of us to date this week." I looked at Lodge with disbelief. "You will have to continue this pattern until you choose one of us to be your boyfriend, Loch. I told you that we would include you, protect you, and that you would be one of us, but in order for that to happen, one of us has to be laying pipe inside you on a regular basis."

Well, there it was. No room left for interpretation.

"Unless you want to just bounce around the team getting fucked," Lodge said hopefully.

"No," I immediately said.

The QB swept the room with his arm. "You have the whole team to pick from again. So, who shall it be?"

"I pick Marcus the freshmen and these two best friends from the senior table . . ."

I was interrupted by Glen who blurted out, "Who? Fucking Pushman and Smida?"

The rest of the table chuckled and Calvin raised his voice. "No fucking way that those two idiots are going to get to hit Loch's sweet ass this week and I'm not!"

"You will abide by the rules, Thomas, or you will not participate at all," Lodge threatened him. "Go on, Loch."

I really didn't know who my second pick would be, so I left the senior table and headed over to the juniors. I smacked Hamilton's face as he looked expectantly up to me. Not seeing anyone that caught my eye, I headed over to the sophomores.

Immediately I locked my gaze onto a big bald-headed stud with black skin so dark that it looked shiny. He was very muscular and tattooed all over. I walked over to him and said, "What's your name, stud?"

"Watkins, defensive end."

"You'll do, Watkins," I announced to the crowd. I heard a collective sigh of disappointment come from them. Looking over to the freshman table, I locked gazes with Marcus and he nodded his approval to me.

"Thanks for dinner, fellas. I look forward to another week of getting to know the team better," I said loudly as I made my way towards the door.

I realized as I escaped that it would be a week before I saw Marcus again because I had stupidly picked upper classmen who would be allowed to go out with me before him. *Oh well, I guess after a week I would know whether he was the one or not.* Or at least, that's what I told myself as I headed back to my dorm.

Chapter Thirteen

Thursday morning as I sat in class, I had a brilliant idea. I sent a text to Lodge and asked him if he could pass along that I wanted to go out with Pushman and Smida both tonight. They were best friends and I was sure they wouldn't mind going out with me at the same time.

The response came immediately from the quarterback that they would both see me after practice. I could kill two birds with one stone and speed up the amount of time between visits by Marcus. I was quite happy with myself, but suddenly felt sick to my stomach. I decided to text Marcus.

Hey buddy, what cha doing?

Thinking about our date in a few days. U?

Speaking of that, I have one tonight with those two seniors and was wondering what you thought I should do . . .

Why should I have any bearing on what you will do, Loch?

Because it matters to me

It shouldn't

But it does

Do you have enough information to make a decision yet?

No

Then you should gather as much info from them as you can . . .

Thanks. I'm looking forward to seeing you soon.

Same

I was a little irritated at his tone in the text string and re-read it several times as I walked home. When Marcus said that I should *gather info*, did he mean that I was supposed to fuck around with these new guys? Did he expect me to? Would he

94

hate me if I did?

There was no fanfare this time when I had my first date. The guys in my dorm were over it, so I sat on the bench and waited alone. The two very unlikely best friends arrived shortly after six in a Mercedes Benz SLS convertible.

Walking out towards the car, I marveled at the look of these two friends in this very expensive car.

"Loch! Hop in," the small one said to me as he slid out of the front passenger seat and into the small back. He was a kicker and one of the smallest men on the team.

"Nice ride," I said as I sat beside the big lineman who was the kicker's best friend.

"Revis comes from money. I'm poor as shit," Pushman informed me.

"Seems like you are pretty rich to me, for having him as a friend, Pushman."

"Yeah, I am." He smiled and pulled out of the parking lot. The wind whipped our faces as Pushman floored the powerful engine down the semi-deserted street. There was no way we could talk, so I just enjoyed the ride. Pushman drove out of town and eventually stopped at a Mexican restaurant on the outskirts of Durham.

"You like Mexican?" Pushman asked me as he parked.

"Absolutely."

The food was good and there was no sexual overtures from my two dates, which was refreshing but kept me guessing. It was very obvious that although Smida had the money, Pushman had the brains, so it was no wonder that the two of them made such a great pair. They were both really nice and hoped to be on the same NFL team next year.

I finally just broke down and asked them, "So, you two want to go back to the house and fuck?" I had come to terms with the fact that I was going to need a back-up plan if Marcus fell through, so I was going to have to see what these two guys had to offer.

"Absolutely," Pushman repeated my answer from earlier. Suddenly, I had a thought. "On one condition . . ."

"What?"

"I don't want you talking about it in the locker room," I said as I felt the heat bloom on my neck and ears.

"Done," Pushman agreed.

I looked over at Smida and he said, "We won't."

"Okay, then. Let's go get sweaty," I said.

The three of us arrived at the football booster's house and made our way to the bedroom. Pushman had never been with a marked man before, but true to their opposite natures, Smida had been banging his family's Servants since he had turned thirteen.

After stripping my clothing off, I dropped to my knees at the end of the bed where my boys were sitting. Their bodies could not have been more different, but one thing was almost exactly the same—their cocks. Both friends had skinny dicks that were average in length.

Sucking Pushman's prick into my mouth first, I gave Smida a hand job and then switched back and forth between them. The two friends got hard quickly and each fucked me doggy style until they had filled me with their hot cream.

When I saw that both boys were ready to go again, I asked them if they wanted to try double fucking me. Usually, I would not be a proponent for double fucking since it hurts so much, but both ballers had skinny dicks and were such close friends that I knew they would love for their cocks to be sliding into me together.

Pushman and Smida were crazy for the idea so I showed them what to do. I told the bigger one to lie down on the bed and I lubed his joint up generously. Straddling his thick frame, I lowered myself down on his cock and bounced a few times. I was slick already from the two loads of cum inside me and the extra lube, so I soon leaned forward and wrapped my arms around Pushman's thick neck.

"Okay, Smida, can you see the target?" I asked sarcastically, knowing my ass cheeks were spread wide open and my asshole was on full display, even as it was being stretched open by Pushman's cock.

"I see it," he said with childlike enthusiasm.

"Place your cockhead on top of Pushman's cock right where it goes inside of me," I directed.

"There's no room," Smida said as he sighed.

"You push it into Pushman's shaft and then inside me at the same time," I instructed.

Smida tried several times and was still unable to get it. He got frustrated and gave up.

"I have a different way," I finally said, pulling myself off of Pushman's broad chest.

Making them both lie down on the bed, I interlocked their legs together like two pair of scissors in a battle. I greased their cocks and showed them how to hold the bases of them together for me.

After two attempts, I was able to push my ass down onto their pricks as they penetrated me. Moaning with pleasure, I slid down to the base of the super-cock.

"Holy fuck!" Pushman said in astonishment.

"Feels so fucking tight," Smida said, returning his buddy's enthusiasm.

"It feels like I'm being split wide open," I groaned as I directed them how to support my thighs as I impaled myself over and over on their now thick cock.

It was the first time that I had ever been double penetrated before and I thought to myself that it would probably be a very long time before I ever tried it again. It hurt more than it was pleasurable, but I was glad that I could check it off of my bucket list of sexual positions.

Pushman and Smida couldn't have been any nicer to me. After they collectively reached their climax within seconds of each other, they lay beside me panting and laughing. If I had not met Marcus a few days before, I probably would have picked the two best friends to be my boyfriends and been very happy for the year.

But, now knowing Marcus, I knew that these two football-ers didn't compare to him. I was still waiting to see how he was in bed, but my mind was so full of him that no one else could compare.

Chapter Fourteen

I spent the remainder of Wednesday night soaking in the garden tub of the house that had been used for my recent dates. Pushman and Smida offered to wait around and walk me home, but I insisted that they go without me. I told them that I was going to soak for a few hours, watch some TV in bed, and sleep here tonight.

My ass felt a little better after the soak, but it burned like a father-fucker the next morning when I woke early. Tears actually formed in my eyes as I walked down the stairs of the booster's house to go back to my dorm. Thankfully, the pain started to subside the more I walked and by the time I reached my room in my dorm, it was just a deep ache.

Exhausted from my night, I went to sleep immediately and dreamed of a marked man in a freak show whose cock was split into two. I woke up the next morning still pretty sore.

I had two classes that day in which I alternated standing and sitting. There was no comfort in either. I had considered texting Marcus on my walk back to the dorm at the end of my day, but decided against it. I stopped and grabbed a sub sandwich for lunch and carried it back to the dorm with me. I had quite a bit of homework and a paper due by Monday, so I committed myself to spending the rest of the day on them.

Rounding the corner of the upper quad and starting to criss-cross it to my dorm, I felt a strange pull on me and immediately spotted a stud on the bench that was out of place. A few steps closer and I recognized it as Marcus Battle.

Marcus seemed to spot me and recognize me immediately. He followed every footstep of my path to him with his eyes.

"Hey," he greeted me.

"Hey," I returned, stopping right in front of his knees. "This is a nice surprise."

"Is it?" His golden eyes burned with a fiery intensity that I had rarely seen. "I was afraid that you would think I was overstepping or smothering you."

"What if I want to be smothered by you?" I asked with a suggestively raised eyebrow.

Marcus chuckled and said, "Just studying, Loch. I wanted to know if you wanted to, you know, hang out and study . . . together."

"Sure. I would like that." I held up the sub and asked, "Did you eat already?"

"Yeah, I ate at the training table."

"Then you can watch me eat this sandwich," I said matter-of-factly.

"I hope not suggestively," he said with a raise of his eyebrow and a smirk on his face.

"Would that get me some action?" I asked hopefully.

"Not today, Loch, not today."

"Come on," I said in faux disgust as I unlocked the dorm door and led him upstairs. Marcus threw his backpack on one shoulder and held it there with a big thumb. He emitted powerful sex appeal that was always shocking to me.

"You have no roommate?" he asked in surprise when he saw my room contained one of everything instead of the usual pairs.

"No. I think the University thought it might be better for me that way."

"It's awesome," Marcus said in awe.

"It is," I agreed.

"And you have air conditioning?"

"Doctor's note for my allergies," I explained. "Want something to drink . . . a beer maybe?"

"Not while I'm in season, you lush."

"Sorry, I was just trying to be hospitable."

Marcus cocked his head at me and said, "I noticed you were walking kinda funny. Is that from being too . . . hospitable?"

I laughed out loud and nodded my head. Was he mad? Did he hate me for fucking around with the two seniors last night? Why couldn't I lie to him?

"None of my business," he finally said, holding up his hands in surrender.

"It might be one day," I suggested.

Marcus looked at me. It was then that I knew that I could never hide anything from him. He had some kind of effect on me that I couldn't explain or really even understand. My crotch blazed with fire and my ass started to itch deep inside.

I swallowed hard and asked, "Would you like me to rub your feet again?"

Marcus had taken a seat on the couch and was pulling a book out of his backpack. "You don't mind?"

"No," I said, licking my lips. I tried to reposition my hard cock, so I could walk over to the couch without Marcus noticing, but it was to no avail.

"I guess you don't," he teased as he looked at the tent I was making in my basketball shorts.

"I'm trying not to be so obvious."

Marcus twisted sideways and held up his foot and waved it at me. "I'm flattered and a little intimidated by the size of that thing."

"Please," I scoffed. "I felt yours while I was lying on you the other day and it's even bigger than mine."

Marcus Battle smiled easily at me.

I had never met someone my age that had so much confidence and so much willpower, unfortunately. Sitting down on the couch at his feet, I guided them onto my lap. Marcus was wearing a pair of Nike Zoom Field General tennis shoes in Carolina blue and white.

"Nice shoes," I commented and saw him put a thick finger to his lips. I didn't say anything else, but worked on getting his feet free of his shoes and socks. Once those beautiful feet were revealed, I set my mind on rubbing and massaging them to the best of my abilities.

Watching him out of the corner of my eye, I noticed that Marcus continued to read and didn't seem to notice me rubbing his feet at all. When I was finished, he looked up and said, "Thanks, Loch. That felt really good."

"Welcome," I said, reaching forward and grabbing my laptop. I had decided to write my paper while Marcus was here.

"You're going to use your laptop?"

"Yes."

"You'll sit here," Marcus said firmly, pointing at the space between his legs as he separated them. "If you want to, of course," he added quickly.

"I want to."

"Good."

I kicked off my tennis shoes and slid down the couch towards Marcus. He immediately wrapped me in his arms and legs like a hunky octopus. Marcus' hard cock came into my awareness as I felt it throbbing against my backside through the thin silky material of my shorts.

"Good," he repeated into the back of my hair.

Smiling to myself, I opened the laptop and logged in. I leaned back into Marcus' strong chest and started typing. Normally, I would be totally distracted and not be able to work on my paper at all, but something about Marcus' firm stance released me.

I was able to write a lot of my paper before Marcus started to rub my bare legs with the bottoms of his feet, which totally turned me on and distracted me. His thick hand on my chest moved to the side and pinched my nipple.

"I have to go to practice, Loch. Thanks for letting me hang with you."

"My pleasure . . . and speaking of my pleasure, is there anything I can do for you before you go?" I asked hopefully, not being able to see his face.

"Not today, Loch, not today," he said like a broken record.

I smiled, amazed once again at his willpower and determination. Sliding back down to the end of the couch, I retrieved his socks and shoes and carefully redressed him. Marcus watched me the whole time with a smile on his thin lips.

Once I laced Marcus' last tennis shoe onto his foot, I stood up and he gave me a hug. It was an intimate act that signaled us as more than friends. I melted into his broad chest, noticing the heat rolling off of his body and an incredible smell of man that made me almost delirious.

"See you soon, Loch."

"I hope so," I said, flirting.

He waved before turning and slipping out of the door. From the window, I watched him emerge from my dorm and head across the quad to South Campus. He walked with swagger and purpose. I knew that I needed to be with him soon or I was going to go insane. Never had I wanted to fuck with someone so badly.

Almost as if he felt my presence at the window, Marcus reached the end of the quad, turned around, and saluted me with two fingers. I waved back as he disappeared behind a brick wall.

I went back to my homework, only stopping occasionally to remember a conversation or a touch that I had just experienced with Marcus. I was so relieved that he wasn't mad at me for fucking Pushman and Smida and so happy that he had stopped by to spend time with me, that I had a smile plastered on my face even as I read my history text.

CHAPTER FIFTEEN

The next day, I was in a foul mood from the second that I rolled out of bed. It wasn't until I was eating lunch by myself in the dining hall that I figured out that my bad mood was because I was dreading my date tonight with Watkins.

Not because I had anything against Watkins, but I wanted to spend my night with Marcus or my friends instead. *Suck it up, Brand. It is one dinner and maybe a hot fuck afterwards.*

Watkins picked me up in an older model Mazda and drove me to a really nice restaurant overlooking Franklin Street. It was by far the nicest of all the places my dates had taken me. Dinner was delicious, but Watkins was totally distracted by his phone the entire meal. He would ask me about myself and then get distracted by a call or a text.

When dinner was over, I had pretty much already decided that I was not interested in fucking around with him. I knew he was not the man for me. I ordered dessert while he was on a call in the hallway and finished it before he even returned.

Watkins walked up to the table and asked, "Ready to go?"

"Sure," I answered as I handed him the check.

He paid on the way out and drove directly to the booster's house without even asking me if I wanted to go. Once he parked in the driveway, I got up the courage to tell him what I was thinking.

"I'm pretty tired, Watkins. I think I kinda just wanna go back to my room and crash."

Watkins pleaded, "No way! Come in for just a drink."

I felt bad that I was cutting the date short, so I agreed. "But just one, Watkins and then I am going to go."

"Yeah, that's right," Watkins said, putting an arm around my shoulders and heading for the door.

I heard noise in the house as we stepped on the porch. The door was unlocked already and when Watkins pushed the door open—there was a full-fledged party going on.

Watkins excitedly high-fived the boys inside and someone handed him a solo cup. "These are my buds!" he yelled over the noise of the cheering and the loud music.

I was smart enough to not step inside the door, standing on the threshold instead.

The cheering died down and an older guy approached me, completely eyeing me up and down. "Is this the fine piece of ass that we're going to fucking pound to pieces tonight?" The alcohol fumes coming out of his mouth were almost intolerable.

I turned to Watkins, waiting for him to defend me, and when he didn't, I answered firmly, "No, it is not!"

The guy swung immediately and slapped me hard across the face. "No one's asking you, cock whore," he snarled.

It felt like my cheek was exploding and I pressed my hand to it like that would help. I felt the tears form in my eyes. All talking had stopped in the house and a crowd was forming.

Watkins smiled and put his arm around the guy who looked like he was in his late twenties. "Damien, man. He's going to put out for all of us. We just gotta chill is all . . ."

Damien glared at me and then said loudly, "That's right! That bitch is gonna spread his legs and get fucked by every dirty dick in this joint!" The crowd cheered.

"Like hell," I said as I turned and bolted. Damien tried to grab and stop me, but I was too determined. Kicking and yelling at anyone who touched me, I escaped, jumped from the porch, and ran out of the gate. I could hear them chasing me, but once I was off of the property they seemed to give up.

Slowing to a jog, I watched behind me, making sure that I wasn't being followed and that's when I ran into someone. The collision almost knocked the wind out of me, but thanks to the other person bracing themselves against my arms, it didn't.

I smelled him before seeing him in the growing dark. "Marcus?"

"Loch, are you okay?" His voice was deep and reassuring like a lighthouse in the middle of a storm.

"I am now," I said as I relaxed into his chest.

"You are shaking. Come sit down." Marcus pulled me into a side street over to the low stone wall that divided much of the campus from the streets. He sat down and I stood in front of him.

"What are you doing here?" I asked in confusion.

"Sit," he commanded as he patted his thighs.

Moving his knees together, I straddled his lap and sat on his long legs facing him.

He was a little startled by my closeness and he stuttered, "I . . . was just . . . coming to check on you."

"Really?"

"I know it sounds totally creepy, but Watkins has a certain reputation and I was worried about you."

I snuggled into his arms, put my head against his chest, and let out a big sigh. "I'm glad you did."

"Tell me what happened," he ordered. His tone had turned suddenly very serious.

I told Marcus the story, feeling his anger swell inside him the more I talked. His eyes narrowed.

"You are very brave. I'm quite proud of you," he finally said, after I had finished my story.

I pulled back from the freshmen footballer and stared into his eyes, made dark by the night, but still reflecting the nearby street lamp. Reaching up, I touched Marcus' face and ran my hand down his strong jaw, feeling the stubble of his day's growth of hair. This moment was electric and the connection between us was indescribable.

"What color would your beard be if you grew it out?" I suddenly asked.

"Kinda dark copperish," he said, smiling. "Why?"

"Would you grow it out for me ... if I was your boyfriend?"

Marcus didn't hesitate. "A lot of things would grow ... if you were my boyfriend."

"Marcus Battle, I would like to be your boyfriend, if you will have me," I said, feeling a little queasy as I said the words.

"I would be glad to have you," he said, his deep voice rumbling through me. "But you haven't even let me fuck you, yet, Loch," he teased me.

"Don't remind me," I groaned.

"You won't be disappointed," he said gruffly, with a huge grin spreading across his face.

Holy fuck! Does that mean that he isn't horribly deformed? What does he mean that I won't be disappointed? Suddenly very excited, I asked, "Can we do it now?"

"Not today, Loch, but I am enjoying being close to you. Would you like me to sleep over?"

"Hell, yes! Let's go!" I practically jumped off of his lap and grabbed his arm to drag him towards my dorm. It was too hard to contain my enthusiasm so I didn't even try.

"Slow down, big boy," Marcus said, laughing as he lumbered after me.

Fortunately, we were very close to my dorm.

"You tired?" Marcus asked me once we were locked inside my dorm room. He had to be out of his fucking mind to ask me that question.

"I'm very excited right now," I snorted as I thrust my hips forward and made my hard-on even more evident than it already was.

"I see that," he said drolly. "I mean, do you want to watch some TV or go to bed?"

"And there really won't be any sex?"

"No. We will fuck when I say so, Loch."

Jesus, I loved when he said things like that. "Are you going to say so tonight or tomorrow morning, Marcus?"

"No."

I tried to hide my disappointment. "Then can we lie in bed and watch TV?"

"Sure."

I stripped to my underwear and watched Marcus do the same thing. He was wearing a pair of Reebok black and blue boxer briefs that made the muscles on his legs pop and I couldn't take my eyes off of the bulge in the front it.

Marcus growled, "Don't even think about it, Loch. Understand?"

"Yes, Marcus. Contrary to popular belief, we marked men can control ourselves."

"Really?" Marcus smirked.

"Most of the time," I admitted, my bravado crumbling. His large hands reached the hem of his t-shirt and pulled it up. I was stunned by the sight of his chest. He was more developed than I had first thought and he had the smallest little nipples on top of his meaty pecs. The top of Marcus' chest was covered in a light dusting of dark copper-colored hair. His belly button was partially an outie.

"Okay. I'm not going to be able to control myself now," I admitted flatly, licking my lips.

"You are really into me?" Marcus asked in surprise.

"Good lord, I know you are a football player, but you can't be that thick can you?"

"I can be pretty thick," he informed me with another smirk and a grab of the outline of his cock in his underwear.

"Fuck me!" I said almost breathlessly.
"Not tonight, Loch, not tonight."

CHAPTER SIXTEEN

After turning the air conditioner on high, I spent the rest of the night snuggled into Marcus Battle's chest and arms. Eventually falling asleep, I dreamed of a bronze statue that came to life, captured me, and held me impaled on his big copper joint so I couldn't run.

I woke up feeling better than I had felt in a long time. My bed smelled like Marcus and my mind was full of him. I reached behind me and found the bed to be empty.

Where the hell is Marcus? Did he leave already?

My questions were answered in less than a minute when a moist Marcus walked into my room wearing nothing but one of my bath sheets. I caught myself staring with my mouth wide open.

"Thanks for letting me stay, Loch."

"My pleasure," I replied with a yawn.

Marcus started to pull his shorts on while still wearing the towel. "I gotta run. Time to work out."

"Will we still get to go out tomorrow?" I asked hopefully.

"I want to, don't you?" he asked, pulling his t-shirt down over his broad chest.

"I do. May I put your shoes on for you, Marcus?"

He looked at me oddly for a few seconds and said, "Yeah, man." Marcus sat down on the couch and turned sideways into our now-familiar position. I sat on the edge of the couch, wiped my new boyfriend's feet dry, and put his socks and shoes back on him. I enjoyed this intimacy that we had shared several times almost more than just being around Marcus.

"I didn't realize how intense it would be . . ." he said softly.

I looked deeply into those golden eyes of his and asked, "What?"

"I never had a . . . been in a situation like this before."

"Well, you could've fooled me." I chuckled. "You're doing almost everything right, Marcus." I gave him a withering look and repeated, "Almost everything."

"I know it's been hard . . ."

"I've been hard for quite some time," I said dryly.

"I don't want you to grow bored with me," he finally admitted. The vulnerability in his voice was heart-wrenching.

"What's the reason you came to check on me tonight, Marcus?"

"I felt like you might need me."

"And I did. We have some kind of connection." I watched him nod his head in agreement.

He swallowed hard. "Do you usually have that with your . . . boyfriends?"

"Never."

Marcus smiled broadly as he shook his shaggy head at me. "Good." He disappeared with a wave of his hand and I didn't see him again until the night of our date. I was hoping that he was going to come back every night and sleep with me, but it didn't happen. He sent me a text on Sunday morning.

Are you available to start our date early, since it is a school night?

I am. Can't wait to see me?

Honestly, yes. LOL

Same. What do you want to do?

Fuck.

I paused. He's finally going to let himself fuck around with me?

But we can't . . . yet.

Fuck! What was it going to take to get me in this man's pants?

Soon, maybe?

111

Soon. I thought about going to the movies.

Sounds good. I could blow you while you watch if the theater is dark enough.

You could blow me even if the lights are on high, wink wink.

Not today, Marcus, not today!

Haha! You're gonna pay for that!

I hope that I will have to pay with my ass!

Careful!

I borrowed a car. Be on the sidewalk behind your dorm in sixty seconds.

Yes, sir!

Holy fuck! That was a term used by Servants for their Masters. I had to admit that I loved it when Marcus commanded me and the fact that I just called him by that title made my balls ache with desire for him. I had never used that title with anyone before and honestly never thought I ever would. But here it was, just rolling off of my fingers.

Hurrying downstairs, I made it to the sidewalk within seconds of Marcus' arrival. "I'm glad you didn't make me wait," Marcus said, smirking at me as I got into the car. I could feel our sexual and electrical pull from the moment the car stopped.

"I wouldn't waste a second of your time," I replied, smirking back.

"Don't think I didn't notice how you signed off on that last text string."

"I like that you notice everything."

We both chuckled as Marcus pulled into traffic. The car already smelled like him. The movie was really good, even if Marcus didn't let me give him a blow job in the darkened theater. Towards the end of the movie, he put a thick hand on the inside of my thigh. I enjoyed running my fingers over his strong hand and wrist in exploration.

My cock was hard as a rock as we left the movies, making it hard to walk without it being noticeable.

"Why is your cock always so hard?" Marcus asked with genuine curiosity as we walked to the car.

"Hello? Can't you see what you do to me?"

"How? I'm not even doing anything . . ."

"You don't have to. I can just feel you and then you grab my thigh and it just kinda over stimulates me."

"I didn't mean to over stimulate you."

"I love it," I admitted to him.

"What do you mean you can feel me?"

I shrugged at first, but under his withering stare, I felt compelled to tell him. "It's weird. When you are near me, I can sense your presence. It feels like I can read your emotions and thoughts. I know your desires and wishes."

"I feel the same thing," he simply said. "I've never felt anything like it."

"Me either." Changing the subject, I asked, "What do you want to do now?"

"I want to take you back to your room and fuck your brains out," he said with a completely serious face and tone of voice while he started to drive away from the theater.

"I'm in!" I said excitedly. "Well, you'll be in, but I'm all for it!"

Marcus sighed as he parked outside of my dorm.

"But I know we can't do it yet," I said in resignation.

He looked at me, shocked to hear me say those words. "Why not?"

"Because, Marcus, it needs to be perfect and it will only be perfect for you when you know it is the right time. No matter how much I want to suck your thick cock and ride it to Charlotte and back, I'm not going to jeopardize that."

"You are making me so fucking hot." He looked at me with new respect and said, "Wow! You are amazing."

"What will be amazing, if I can make it up the stairs of my dorm with this painful hard-on," I asked, starting to laugh.

"I can carry you." He smirked.

"That would make it worse," I commented while I got out of the car. We walked up to my room and I locked us inside.

"What do you want to do?" Marcus asked me.

"I want to get naked and lie in bed with you," I said softly, blushing to my roots.

"All right, but I'm going to keep my underwear on."

"I'm not," I said matter-of-factly.

Marcus held me in his big arms against his big chest as we watched football on TV. I wasn't even sure what was happening in the game because I was so distracted by his nearly naked body and the rock hard throbbing cock poking me in my back.

"I wanna see you jerk off," Marcus growled into my ear. His voice was lusty with need.

"Really?" I asked, stunned.

"Yeah. Your cock has been so hard for so long, it needs relief."

"So does yours." I noticed my voice was far huskier than usual.

"I'll take care of myself later."

Marcus was the most stubborn man I had ever met. "You sure?"

"Yes." Marcus reached around my chest and pinched both of my nipples hard between his long rough fingers. "It's an impressive cock, Loch."

"Thanks." I groaned. Arching my back and closing my eyes, I wrapped a hand around my hard shaft and began to pump it back and forth.

"Tell me what you are thinking about, Loch."

Why does he make me say these things to him? "You."

He pinched my nipples harder as he constantly rubbed them—twisting the hard nubbins between the pads of his fingertips. "What about me?"

I was close to my release and my breathing became shallow. "I'm imagining you on top of me instead of always under me. Your huge cock penetrating me, stretching my hole wide. Your body holding me down. Your eyes blazing at mine. Your smell permeating my nose. The taste of your sweet cum in my mouth. My ears hearing you grunt and groan as you thrust deeper and harder into me than anyone ever has before—" I broke off as I shot my load.

My hot cum splashed on my chest and neck with some force. It felt like it had come straight up from my balls in a single blast, and there was more to follow. Marcus held onto my sides as I spasmed from my climax. I continued to jack my cock as I bucked on top of my new boyfriend.

"Fuck," Marcus said, his voice full of awe. "Do you always have such big loads?"

"Not usually," I answered, chuckling. I wiped myself with my underwear. Turning, I flipped onto my stomach and lay over Marcus. "Are you sure that I can't at least do the same thing for you?"

"Soon, Loch, soon. I think I might explode if it's not soon!"

CHAPTER SEVENTEEN

Marcus and I spent a great night in my room. I made Kraft Mac and Cheese on my hotplate and roast beef sandwiches from my fridge. I loved sleeping with Marcus' hot body beside me and I especially loved how my bed smelled the next morning, just like him. He got up early and showered without me again.

I got a text from Daniel Lodge while Marcus was in the shower.

Hey guy
Hey Lodge. Whatup?
You need to come by after practice today
What for?
To make four more picks, unless you have decided and in that case you need to tell us your decision
Okay. Six?
Yeah, six. See you then!

"I have to be at the end of your practice today," I told Marcus when he came back to my room from the shower.

"Cool," he said nonchalantly. "I think the boys on your floor are getting used to seeing me in the shower. They must think I am fucking your brains out every night."

"I wish," I said with a snort.

He got serious as he pulled his shorts on under his towel. "Do you know what you are going to do after practice today?"

I looked into his golden eyes and licked my lips in response to his naked nearness. "You still wanna be my boyfriend, right?"

"Absolutely!"

Thank God! "Then I'm going to tell them that I have found someone and that you are him."

He whistled. "They are not going to like that."

"Who cares? If you like it and I like it, then that is all that matters." I was displaying a bravado that I wasn't sure that I actually felt.

Marcus looked at me through his wet bangs and I saw vulnerability on his face for the first time. "You are still not sure that you like it."

"I know that I like you. I know that I like how I feel when you are with me. I hope that I will love the way you taste in my mouth, the way you feel inside my ass, and the way you fuck me. I'm willing to wait for that until you are ready."

"I hope that you won't be disappointed."

I could see the shadow of doubt cross his face. "I trust you, Marcus. If there was some reason that I wouldn't be happy, you would tell me, wouldn't you?"

"I would."

"Good. Then we are settled."

"You're a brave man, Loch. I'm in awe of you most days."

"You'll be in all of me all the time soon," I said laughing.

"Jesus, I can't wait," he said, as he pulled on his t-shirt.

"Me either," I said exaggeratedly as I fell back on the bed in a spread-eagled position.

"I'm going to work out. I'll see you after practice, Loch."

"See ya, Marcus. Thanks for my date last night."

"Yeah, no problem," he said with a grin as he left my room.

I watched him out the window and he waved to me at the end of the quad again. What was I going to do with him? What if I didn't like his cock or the way he fucked? Could our connection be enough to get us through it? I could teach him how I liked it since we would have four years together . . .

I guess I was about to find out. Classes drug that morning and I couldn't help but come back to my room in the afternoon and jack off to Marcus' smell all over my bed. Wallowing around on it, I breathed in deeply of his sweat and musk from the sheets and pillowcase as I whacked my hard cock. I came in another huge explosion of hot semen and then sadly stripped the bed and changed the sheets.

Six o'clock came a lot faster than I had wanted, but I was ready in the locker room when the football team arrived from practice. All of my favorites greeted me and Watkins glared at me from across the room. Lodge gathered everyone together and got them quiet.

"So, Loch, you have been on several dates with many members of our great team . . ." There was a cheer from the players that interrupted him. "Have you made a decision yet about which one of us you will belong to?"

"I have made a decision about which one I would like to be my boyfriend," I answered his question while correcting him.

A groan came up from the crowd, who was obviously disappointed that most of them were not going to get a chance to try out for the position.

"And your decision?"

"I have chosen . . . Marcus Battle," I said loudly.

Excited chatter ran through the crowd. "A freshman?" Lodge asked in surprise.

"He hasn't even fucked Loch yet!" Calvin yelled at Daniel Lodge, his face an angry mask of pain.

"Is that true, Loch?" Daniel asked as the crowd quieted to hear my answer.

I firmly planted my feet for support and said, "It doesn't matter if it is true or not. I have asked him to be my boyfriend and he has accepted."

"Fish, get up here!" Lodge called to the back of the locker

room. The players parted as Marcus made his way up front. His head was down and he was muddy and sweaty from practice. He looked like he had been run over.

"Is this true, fish? Have you agreed to be Loch's boyfriend without even fucking him?"

"I have," Marcus said loudly and firmly while looking up for the first time. The players were getting their first view of the confident commanding presence that Marcus could have.

I watched with glee as Daniel actually took a tiny step back in response to Marcus' new demeanor.

Marcus continued, "Loch and I are a pair now and therefore deserving of your respect and protection."

Daniel had recovered and agreed by saying, "Marcus is correct. Now that Loch has chosen, he is entitled to our respect and protection. He is one of us now, or at least he will be once Battle has done the dirty deed and fucked him silly."

"It will be soon," Marcus promised, igniting the burn in my balls.

The players grunted their consent and a few of them welcomed me to the team. To their credit, most of them smacked Marcus on the arm or chest bumped him as they said their congratulations. The players seemed to have a newfound respect for him and that was something he was not used to.

When the hoopla died down, Marcus turned to me and said, "Go home. Work on your paper that is due on Wednesday and I will be by later with dinner."

I narrowed my eyes at him and asked, "How do you know I have a paper due on Wednesday?"

He shrugged and said, "I looked at your desk calendar this morning." When I shook my head at him slightly, he asked, "What? I need to know everything about you."

"Everything?"

"Everything," he said, grinning broadly. "Now, go work on that paper while I shower and get dinner."

"See ya," I said, excited that I was going to get to see him again tonight.

"Careful," he warned me. Whether it was of others or to watch my behavior towards him, I was unsure. I pondered the meaning of his warning all the way back to my dorm, but quickly put it out of my head as I started writing the paper I needed for Wednesday's Psych 101 class. I had just finished exploring the differences between Jungian and Freudian when Marcus tapped on my door.

"Hey," I said as I opened the door wider to let him in.

"Hi. Someone left the front door propped open. I closed it and brought us Subway."

"Concerned about my safety, Marcus?"

"Always." He grunted.

"Perfect," I said as I grabbed two Cokes out of the mini-fridge. We sat down on my couch and ate off of the coffee table. I turned on the news and very little was said between us as we quickly ate the chips and sandwiches he had brought over.

"I didn't know what you would like . . ." Marcus explained.

"It's good," I said as I ate. "So, how do you think I did?" I finally asked him as I threw away our trash.

"In the locker room?"

"Yes," I said, rolling my eyes at him.

He stared at me in disbelief and then asked, "Did you just roll your eyes at me?"

"Sorry, I did," I said, laughing.

"Well, well, well. I was going to give you this as a surprise because I was so proud of how you did, but now I'm not so sure." As he said this, I watched as he pulled something out of his shorts pocket and covered it between his closed hands.

"What is it?" I asked excitedly. I had always loved presents.

Marcus tilted his head down and looked at me through his

shaggy bangs. "What do you say?"

"I'm sorry for rolling my eyes at you, sir." I tried to say it contritely, but it just came across as sarcasm.

"You better be," my new boyfriend growled with a lusty smile on his face.

"Tell me what it is, Marcus," I whined. When he shook his head, I jumped onto his lap and tried to get it myself. Marcus let me know who was in charge by refusing to let me pry his hands apart.

"I will tell you when I decide, Loch," he smirked.

I stood up in disappointment, but then had an idea. I reached down between his legs towards his cock.

"You wouldn't dare!" Marcus hissed.

"Try me!" I shot back.

We stared into each other's eyes for what felt like an hour. It was an old-fashioned standoff. Finally, he broke.

"I've decided that I am ready to show you," Marcus said slowly, "in the interest of not wasting any more time."

"Well played, Battle, well played," I complimented him.

He nodded and held his clam-shelled hands out to me. I touched the tops of them as I resumed sitting down on his legs, feeling the electrical charge between us in my balls. I opened his hands and there inside were the keys to the football booster's house.

Touching the keys, I looked up into his golden eyes and asked, "Does this mean what I think it does, Marcus?"

"Yes. It's time."

CHAPTER EIGHTEEN

Marcus and I didn't say a word to each other as we departed my dorm room and headed together to the football booster's house. We were practically running by the time it came into view. Marcus held the sidewalk gate open for me as I ran ahead to unlock the door.

My hands were shaking and I fumbled the keys several times before I got the door open. I slipped inside and Marcus' big frame followed me. Rounding on him and putting both of my palms against his chest, I pushed Marcus into the door, closing it and pinning him against it. Invisible winds swirled the golden sands inside his eyes as they blazed at me. I locked the door and simultaneously Marcus dropped his basketball shorts and jock.

What I saw next in that dim light of the hallway lamp was one of the most amazing sights I had ever experienced. Marcus' cock rose immediately up from his crotch into the small space between us. All of my fears about him being deformed evaporated in a heartbeat. His cock was magnificent.

Marcus' cock was so long and so wide that it couldn't even straighten up fully. It arched from a nest of dark copper pubic hair, unable to fully extend as it hardened. The wide shaft was covered in bulging veins, carrying blood to the end where a huge apple-shaped cock head capped it off. There was a single drop of golden man-nectar on the piss slit that seemed to radiate some type of inner light. I had never seen such a giant sword before and I almost stopped breathing when I realized that it was going to be inside of me before the night was out.

Finally, able to pry my gaze off of his magnificent member

for a second, I looked up at Marcus, whose face wore a look of worry. I smiled a huge fucking grin and watched as his face relaxed. He raised his hand and lowered it onto the top of my head. He pushed down and I knew what to do, because it was what I wanted to do.

Lowering myself to the carpeted floor, I kneeled in front of my new boyfriend and came face to face with his cock. The smell was amazing — masculine and clean like soap. Closing my eyes and breathing in deeply, I imagined a golden light surrounding me and angels singing.

Marcus reached down, grabbed my hands, and put them on the base of his cock. I immediately ran them all over his glorious joint. It was so hard and yet the skin was so soft. Pulling on his hairy ball sack, I inspected his big balls and ran my thumb up the bottom vein of his shaft.

Marcus moved his hand from the top of my head to the back of my head and urged me forward. I closed the gap between us quickly, licking the drop of pre-cum off of his cock head. He tasted delicious and I positioned my hands at the base of his lead pipe while I licked the super-smooth and soft skin of his glans. The taste of his skin was as intoxicating as Marcus' smell was and I felt the familiar electrical charge between us when we touched.

Not being able to stand it anymore, I took Marcus' cock head into my mouth and sucked on it like a *Tootsie Pop*. Marcus sighed deeply as I finally let him inside my hot mouth and his body relaxed into the door. Running my tongue all around the flange where his head connects to his shaft, I left no patch of delicious skin uncovered.

I explored his piss hole with my tongue, forming into a point to try to get inside it. I was rewarded with a steady stream of golden pre-cum that started to flow out of my man and down my throat. Marcus moaned and spread his thighs slightly to increase the experience. He grabbed both sides of my head with rough hands and urged me forward again.

I let him direct me. Relaxing my jaw, I let him slide more and more of himself inside of me. Starting to gag as Marcus' beautiful cock head hit the back of my throat, I pulled off of him. I was ashamed that I could only suck about three quarters of him into my mouth and covered it by licking and sucking the outside of his shaft from tip to balls on all sides.

Trying again, I impaled myself on Marcus' huge rod until I gagged. This time I held onto his hips and contented myself with taking long, hard pulling draws on his cock that hollowed out my cheeks. He responded positively to this treatment and let several deep-throated moans escape from his throat.

My saliva steadily flowed out of the sides of my mouth as I sucked Marcus better than I had ever cared to blow anyone before. I wanted to please him so much that it made my heart hurt that I couldn't do a better job.

Marcus Battle didn't seem to mind at all as he held my head on each side and his whole body quivered before me. I recognized it instantly as a precursor for a climax, so I pulled my head back until nothing but his big apple cock head was in my mouth.

Marcus came in a violent shaking orgasm as I sucked and licked his cock head. He filled my mouth with his sweet cream, sending volley after volley of scalding cum into the back of my throat. I swallowed fast to keep from choking. Even with all of my preparations, Marcus' man-seed still ran down my chin in a steady stream.

He groaned above me as his body continued to convulse. I held onto Marcus' hips to steady him while he used my mouth to thrust into several more times, each thrust producing another ropy strand of earthy cum for me to swallow.

Finally, my boyfriend stilled somewhat and I set about to licking up and down his magnificent shaft to clean him of any lingering evidence of his climax. Once clean, I sucked on the sensitive tip of his cock, coaxing more pearls of cum from his piss hole. I enjoyed listening to Marcus breathing like a horse and when I heard him starting to regain his composure, I twisted my head so that I could look up at him even while keeping his cock inside my mouth. I knew that this drove NOMARs crazy and I did it just to enflame him.

That's when it occurred to me that his climax had not impacted his over-sized dick at all. Marcus was still just as hard and stiff as he was when we walked through the door, and I looked up at him in wonder. He opened his eyes, somehow knowing that I was looking at him, and leaned down to look at me. I recognized the same look of wonder on his face and then his small mouth turned into a huge fucking grin.

He slipped one of his hands off the side of my head and on to my face. Marcus pulled his thick cock out of my mouth and then traced my lips with his fingertip before hooking my mouth with his thumb. I sucked on his rough joint as he pulled me into a standing position with it.

Once we were standing in front of each other, Marcus wrapped his long arms around me and hugged me to him. I returned the gesture and felt the heat pouring off of his big body. We were both sweating profusely, so I grabbed the hem of his t-shirt and lifted it off of him when he let me go. He did the same for me before reaching down and stripping off my basketball shorts and boxer briefs.

I knew what this meant and I was more ready for it than I ever imagined that I could have been. Reaching down to my discarded shorts, I pulled a bottle of lube from the pocket that I had been smart enough to stow away in there as we were leaving. I didn't even know if Marcus' cock would fit inside my tight ass, but I knew it certainly wouldn't without a significant amount of grease on it.

Marcus spun me around in his arms and bent me over. I

placed my hands on the carpet and went down to my knees. My new boyfriend used this position to inspect my puckered hole – running his rough fingertip over it while spreading out my ass cheeks to allow him more access.

The lube was cold and thick when the big footballer squirted it onto the top of my ass crack and moved it down to my hole with two thick fingers. When he pushed those fingers onto my pud and my anal ring spread to allow them access, it took my breath away. If I had thought that there was some type of electrical connection between Marcus and me before, I had not felt anything compared to the lightning storm that was occurring between us at this moment. Marcus' fingers inside me felt like some dicks I had experienced before, and he certainly knew how to use them to loosen me up.

My new boyfriend added another long finger inside me and I moaned my pleasure loudly and unabashedly. I was so ready to be fucked that when Marcus pulled his fingers out of me and walked around to the front of me, I was staring at him in disbelief and confusion. He leaned over and pulled me to a standing position again.

Handing me the lube, he lay down on his back on the carpet in the entrance hallway and held his hard cock up to me. I knelt beside him and generously lubed his hot member while it throbbed in my palm. Once I was satisfied, I straddled Marcus' prone form and smiled down at him.

He returned my smile, but also indicated with a twirl of his finger that he wanted me to turn around. I narrowed my eyes at him when I realized that he wanted me to face away from him. I had waited for this moment longer than I had ever waited for anything in my life and he wasn't even going to let me look at him while I impaled myself on his cock?

Swallowing my disappointment, I turned around and knelt over his thighs. Marcus pushed on my back and I leaned forward over his legs. He played with my rosebud, eventually sticking both of his thumbs inside of it and spreading me wide open. He removed one thumb and soon replaced it with his huge cock head. Marcus pushed it inside of me as he removed his thumb. I stopped breathing as my anal ring spread almost to its limits as it expanded to accommodate that giant cock head. Once the flange cleared my asshole, there was some relief and I started to breathe again.

Marcus, as if sensing my consternation, rubbed my spine and back with one big hand as I slowly relaxed again. He spread his legs and moved mine forward and inside of his. I wasn't sure where he was going with this, so I just concentrated on pushing myself further down on him. Inch after inch, I was able to move him further and further inside my anal channel. The big bulging veins of my new lover's shaft caused minuet sensations to my anal ring as it compressed tighter and tighter around his big unit.

I was determined not to disappoint my new boyfriend in this department. Maybe I couldn't get all of him inside my mouth, but I was definitely going to get him completely in my ass. My determination waivered for a moment as a sharp shooting pain reared its ugly head—like a red-hot knife digging in my bowels. Pain shot through every nerve in my whole body as I pushed myself further down on his fuck stick.

Marcus groaned deeply behind me with what I hoped was pleasure and not pain. The house was getting darker and another lamp in the study beside us clicked on automatically, enveloping us in yellow light. Feeling with my hand, I knew that I only had one more big push to go and he would be all the way inside, but I was unsure if I could do it. I was already feeling so full and it felt like there was no more room inside me at all.

As if Marcus could sense that I could go no further, he reached around me, grabbed my sweaty chest with his huge paw and pulled me back to him. Suddenly it hit me what he was doing. He was recreating our favorite position, with me lying on him, that we had used either to study or watch TV.

Now I was even more desperate to have him fully inside of me. Marcus was a romantic and he deserved all of me. I made contact with his sweaty chest and reached down on either side of him and grabbed his hips. Holding onto them tightly, I pulled myself down hard and felt the last few inches of his throbbing pike enter me.

Marcus hissed between clenched teeth and I let out a huge breath of relief. My ass felt like I was being fucked by a fence post, but that post was all the way inside of me. Marcus' cock had punched my prostate on the way in and now was just manhandling it, sending waves of pleasure coursing through my body.

I lay back and relaxed — feeling like my job was done—and let Marcus take over. He burrowed his knees between mine and then spread his legs, which also spread mine. Planting his large feet on the floor, he partially pulled his hot cock out of me and then thrust it back inside. He started slowly and then built to an incredible pace where he was destroying my asshole as it desperately slid up and down his hard shaft. No one would have been able to tell that I was in pain, because my cock was rock hard and was constantly smacking me on the stomach as Marcus thrusts jarred me each time.

Marcus came again in a torrent of cum that coated and soothed my burning hole. My climax followed quickly behind his as I unleashed a tsunami-sized load onto my chest and stomach. Breathing heavily, I felt the muscles of my ass constrict even further and then heard Marcus grunt. I wondered if he was concerned that my ass was strangling his manhood, because I kinda was.

I loved that Marcus had fucked me in what I considered our favorite position and I was super-impressed by his stamina, but he was apparently just getting started.

CHAPTER NINETEEN

Marcus pushed me to a standing position, causing his huge phallus to be pulled from my tight sphincter. It was a strange feeling to go from complete fullness to complete emptiness and even though having his cock out of my ass relieved the pressure and pain of being stretched wide open, I didn't like it. Marcus stood up behind me and put his big hands on my shoulders. Slowly he began to massage my shoulders until I became very aware of his still-hard prick poking me in the buns and lower back.

I reached behind me and felt for his cock. It was just as hard and hot as it had been two climaxes ago when we first started. I stroked his long shaft and pinched the apple-shaped cock head, causing slimy goo to coat my fingers. I was more than impressed with his virility and when he led me in front of him to the stairs, I readily let him.

The big footballer motioned for me to lie down on the bottom stairs on my stomach. I was grateful that these stairs had a carpet runner going down the middle of the entire staircase. Marcus positioned my hands onto opposite balusters and I gripped them tightly as I prepared to have my ass assaulted again. Marcus lubed himself again and stood on the stair that my knees were resting upon. He bent down and then pulled my head to the side.

As I sought out Marcus' golden eyes in his darkened face, I realized that he was checking with me to make sure I was okay. I nodded in response to his unanswered question and grinned broadly at him. He returned my smile and then fed his cock back into my sore hole.

This time he was in charge and he smoothly guided his steel sword into my sheath until it was buried to the hilt inside of me. It was easier this time, but still really tight. We both groaned loudly as Marcus started to fuck back and forth inside of me. I wished I could have seen him crouch over my ass and fucking destroy it, but once again, my new footballer boyfriend had chosen a position that kept me from seeing him.

Marcus fucked in long slow strokes this time, working in an arc that drove his cock fully inside me with each stroke as it pushed me forward slightly. He continued this pattern until he had almost reached another climax. The closer he got to falling over the edge of his climax, the faster his thrusts became.

I moaned shamelessly as he coated my sore ass with another fresh coat of sticky man goo. Where did all of the cum go? I couldn't possibly have any room left in my ass for any more.

Marcus breathed heavily into my back, where he had collapsed after my ass had drained another load of man cream from his fuck stick. He absentmindedly ran the tip of his index finger around my broad back, tracing the beads of sweat as they formed paths down my skin.

My man was so still and quiet that I thought he might be done, but I was proven wrong when he pulled off of me suddenly and helped me to my feet. Marcus held me against his sweaty chest as I stood up on shaky legs with him. He pointed to the top of the stairs and I held onto the banister with one arm and his broad shoulders with the other as I attempted to climb the stairs.

Reaching the top stair, Marcus stopped my progress and motioned for me to sit down on the next to last step. I took one look at his amazing cock and realized that he was not done yet. I smiled up to him and he grinned a silly grin and shrugged his shoulders.

The light was better at the top of the staircase and this time Marcus wanted me to watch him give me another one of the most thorough fuckings of my short life. He put my ankles onto his strong shoulders and bent me in half like an Olympic gymnast. Bracing himself several steps below me, Marcus pumped his hard joint inside me again. I felt the cooling cum inside my ass start to run out of me as it made room for his magnificent beast again. This time I made sure he was fully invested by reaching down and grabbing each of his ass cheeks and pulling them towards me.

Marcus was surprised at first but then saw what I was do-ing and growled his approval. His ass was slightly furry and even after I had made sure he was fully inside me, I played with and explored his ass cheeks. Eventually, I moved my hands down to the backs of his powerful thighs so that his ass could maneuver to drive that meat missile back and forth through my puckered hole.

Finally, I was getting fucked by Marcus Battle where I could watch him while he worked. His beautiful eyes never left mine as he pile-drove me into that staircase. He opened his mouth and jutted out his strong jaw as he arched his back and delivered one hard thrust deep inside me after another. I ran one hand up his thick chest and pinched his hard, little nipples until he was forced to break eye contact with me, growl at me, and close his eyes.

Letting go of his nipples for a moment, I ran my hand through his damp hair, sweeping the long bangs out of his face. I moved my hand down to his face, feeling the stubble of the day on his jaw and upper lip. Marcus increased the speed of his thrusts causing me to arch my back and writhe in ec-stasy underneath him. My finger fell from his upper lip as he opened his lips.

Tracing my boyfriend's thin lips, I was surprised when he suddenly lurched forward and bit my finger. Marcus kept his perfectly white teeth clamped on my finger as he increased his speed again, sending me into a frenzy of sexual pleasure. My abused asshole was constantly being pushed inwards and then being forced to slide down that thick telephone pole he called a cock only to be pulled back the other way as he pulled that pole back out of me.

My new friend from Ohio's furry belly was scraping the wide vein on the bottom of my hard dick with each thrust, causing me to be completely vulnerable to another orgasm. I moaned and whined underneath him as I shot ropy strands of scalding, strong-smelling spunk between our sweaty bodies.

I was absolutely exhausted. Marcus released my finger from his mouth and I put both hands on the backs of his beefy biceps as I rode out the last of his deep hard thrusts. He came again, filling me with his seed and marking me as his property from now on. There was no doubt in my mind after tonight that I belonged to him for as long as he would have me.

Marcus' cum filled me and warmed from the inside, further evidence of his conquest of me and of his stamina and virility. He continued to mini-thrust his cock into me as he collapsed onto me and I held his broad sweaty chest to me.

When Marcus' breathing returned to normal, he wrapped my arms around his powerful neck and then supported me with his muscular arms around my back. In another amazing feat of strength, especially after having just come four times, the tight end from the football team picked my sore body up into the air as he stood with me.

He walked the last couple of stairs to the top and into the bedroom. His cock twitched and throbbed inside of me as he walked, stimulating me to achieve another hard-on. Marcus placed me down on the soft bed and suddenly noticed my hard cock.

I think he probably was going to withdraw and be done for the night, but when he saw my hardness, he grinned foolishly and was ready for another go. The sore muscles of my back appreciated that I was on a soft bed this time and I watched in awe as he turned me on one side, lifted one leg high into the air and crawled into the saddle between my legs.

Marcus fucked my poor hole like he had never seen it before and like he was a man that needed it to survive. *Maybe he was. Maybe he did.* All I knew was that this man who was my same age, acted and fucked like someone who was much more mature than anyone I had ever met. He knew how to fuck, had just put on the performance of a lifetime, and had the greatest cock that I had ever fucked around with. He was hot as hell, sexy as he could be, and had the potential for a great career as a professional athlete. But more importantly than all of those things, was the fact that he was a great person. He cared about me, he wanted to protect me, he intellectually stimulated me, he was interested in my life, and he satisfied me physically like I had never experienced before. There was some kind of connection between us that was amazing.

I had been watching Marcus' thick hammer sliding between my legs as I was lost in thought, but now I was pulled to look into his eyes. I wondered what he saw when I looked into his eyes. He smiled at me and busted his nut for a fifth straight time in the last two hours. Looking right into his eyes, I saw my life with Marcus unfold inside them and it was a wonderful sight.

CHAPTER TWENTY

I woke up in the middle of the night and realized that Marcus and I had both just collapsed onto the bed after that marathon fuck session and fallen right to sleep. We had not said one single word to each other since entering this house, yet we were connected to each other as significantly as two people could be.

Slipping the covers back, I almost screamed out in pain as I swung my legs over the side of the bed. A sharp shooting pain was radiating out of my ass and it took my breath away with its intensity. I felt filthy, with dried sweat and cum all over me. Taking a deep breath, I carefully began to cross the room where I had to stop and steady myself against the wall by the door.

Marcus was behind me before I even knew he was awake. He held me up and asked, "What's wrong, Loch?"

I swallowed hard and said, "I'm experiencing a little bit of pain."

"We need to go to the hospital?" he asked concerned.

I let him support me and said, "No. Can you just help me back to the bed?"

"Sure." Marcus deposited me back into the big bed. "Where were you going?"

"I was going to get us some bottles of water. I'm parched."

"I'll get it for you." Marcus headed downstairs and returned with four bottles of water. He handed me one and I drained it. I watched him do the same.

He sleepily commented, "You were thirsty."

"We had quite the work out."

"It was fucking amazing," he said. But then he turned serious and said, "But I'm afraid that I've hurt you."

"Marcus, I'm just sore. We did just what I wanted us to do last night. You haven't done anything to me that I didn't want done."

"It's one reason that I made you wait. It's always been difficult for the guys at Service Stations to take my cock and I didn't want it to come between us."

"I couldn't wait for it to come between us. I'm in love with your fucking cock!" I gushed.

"I should have been more careful, but when you took all of me inside, it really turned me on and I went a little bonkers." Marcus sounded very contrite.

I saw his point, but still didn't blame him. "I guess I sent you the wrong message by taking your whole pole."

"I got your message, all right," he said with a chuckle. "Did we fuck four times after you blew me?"

"Yeah," I answered, laughing. "I came twice without touching myself."

"I don't think we said a word the whole time."

"We didn't." I shook my head. "It was the hottest thing that has ever happened to me."

We laughed and then there was an awkward silence. His eyes blazed with lust as he finally admitted, "I'm in love with your ass. And your mouth, Loch."

"I wasn't disappointing?"

"Fuck no! You were everything I dreamed that you could be and more."

"Good. So were you, Marcus. You were amazing." I looked at him in the darkened room with a sense of awe.

"But I hurt you."

"You fucked me hard four times and that hurt me, not you."

Marcus lowered his voice and said, "You were the first person that was able to take all of me on the first try."

"So, you'll keep me?" I asked sleepily, my heart swelling with pride.

"I was just hoping that you hadn't changed your mind about me, since you are hurt." He seemed to hold his breath as he waited for my answer.

"No fucking way," I said with one hundred percent certainty. "Now, come back to bed and sleep. We've got class in the morning."

"I brought this for you," he said softly, holding up a bag of frozen peas.

"You are very sweet." I thanked him as I took the bag and slid it under my burning ass.

"Protecting my investment," he mumbled.

"I'll give you your investment," I growled at him as he crawled into the bed behind me. He chuckled and I fell right to sleep.

Waking in the morning, I rolled over painfully and saw that Marcus wasn't in bed with me anymore, but I could hear him in the shower.

Moments later, my boyfriend walked into the bedroom completely naked and wet, carrying a towel. He was all man, thin and muscled with just a hint of the hairiness that he would be later.

"Marcus," I said breathlessly.

"Loch. You feeling better?" He started to dry himself off.

"I'm feeling good enough to take care of that for you," I said lustfully as I pointed at his glorious cock that was arching out of his crotch at me.

"Really?"

"Marcus, you and I are in this together. You are my boyfriend. If you want a blowjob, you get it. If you want to fuck my ass four times in a row without a break, you get to."

He looked at me with a stern look on his face for a minute before saying, "I don't want to be that guy that constantly takes advantage of you."

"You have to be. That's what a boyfriend does and besides, I'm going to be constantly taking advantage of you as well."

"Well, if you put it like that . . ." Marcus climbed up onto the bed. I turned onto my back with some pain and propped my head up on a couple of pillows.

He was unsure of what to do at first until I patted my upper chest. Carefully straddling me, he hovered above my chest until I told him to sit down. When his ass touched my skin, the familiar electrical charge ran through me and I leaned forward to bury my face in his crotch. I breathed in deeply, loving the clean smell of him.

I lifted his big cock onto my face and sucked his hairy ball sack into my hot mouth. Rolling around his cum makers, I sucked and licked them like they were something to be cherished and worshipped.

Marcus put a big paw on the top of my head and grabbed the top of the headboard with his other one. He rode my insistent mouth like a cowboy on a bronco bull, moaning loudly as I sucked his jewels.

Putting his head forward, he opened his eyes to look down on me and said, "No one's ever done that to me before."

I spit his balls out and said, "I'm going to do things to you that you haven't even imagined were things."

"Now you're just making me hot and when I'm hot, the only place I wanna be is in your tight ass."

"I can make that happen," I said coquettishly.

"Not today, Loch, not today. You have to rest and get better." That look of concern was back on his face.

I'll suck that look right off of his face. I pulled his horse cock down to my mouth and enveloped it in my hot wet hole.

Sure enough, I watched as the concerned look ebbed off of his visage and was replaced with pure rapture. I sucked hard on his big firehose until he was close to his climax and then he took over. Marcus face-fucked me by moving his hips back and forth, driving his cock into my mouth and then back out. He was careful not to choke me, since I still couldn't get him all inside.

"Fuuucccckkkkk!" he groaned through clenched teeth. Marcus Battle came in a huge blast of funky hot cum that flooded my mouth. I swallowed his salty load and let the overflow run out of the sides of my mouth and back onto his thick shaft. Marcus grabbed a fistful of my blond hair and hung on while I continued to milk the sweet cream out of his sensitive organ.

Letting go of me, Marcus arched his head back, breathing deeply. "I won't ever get used to that," he said huskily. He lowered his thick hand down to my face and wiped the trail of cum flowing out of the corners of my mouth as I continued to clean up his throbbing prong. My gaze locked onto his just in time for him to wipe his cum onto my lips with his thumb. I let his cock fall out of my mouth and he replaced it with his cum-covered thumb.

When I sucked his thumb just like I had sucked his cock, Marcus let out a gasp and then a smile appeared on his face. I wondered what he was thinking, but then he told me. He used his thumb to wipe the cum on the other side of my face and fed it to me again.

"Do we get to do this all the time now?" he asked.

"All the time!" I answered, laughing around his thumb. "Anytime we want."

"Fuck! I'm not going to get anything done but this, am I?"

"You are going to do amazing things with your life and so am I," I said confidently. "We are going to study hard, work out, play hard, and fuck like rabbits. We will both be wildly successful."

Marcus raised an eyebrow at me. "Work out?"

"Yes. You have to get much bigger to play better and take the next step and I have to improve my stamina so that I can keep up with you."

"You're going to work out with me?"

"Not today, Marcus, not today, but soon." I cracked up laughing and Marcus stood up off of me.

"I have to go work out now."

"I know. I don't think I'm going to be able to go to class today and I don't think I'm strong enough to walk back to my dorm, so I'm going to stay here and soak in the big tub all day." I looked for his response, knowing that he felt responsible. His face was expressionless. "Can you check on me after your classes?"

"Yes, absolutely. Anything else I can do?"

"Text me on the way over and I'll let you know. You sure you don't mind coming all the way back over here?"

"It's what we do for each other, right?"

I smiled and said, "Yes."

"Then don't worry. I want you better, soon."

"Yes, sir." I watched Marcus get dressed with our clothes that he had brought from the entryway last night. He made sure I had several bottles of water and started to run the bathtub full of hot water before he waved goodbye to me and locked the front door behind him.

How did I get this lucky?

CHAPTER TWENTY-ONE

L ater that day, Marcus came and checked on me just like he had promised. He brought me something to eat and walked back to my dorm with me.

"You are very dependable as a boyfriend, Marcus," I said coyly to him once we were in my room.

"I aim to please," he said with a shake of his shaggy head.

"I need you to please right now," I said quickly.

A shadow of concern crossed his handsome face. "We can't do that. You're recovering."

"I'm ready, my dependable boyfriend," I said teasing him.

"No, not yet."

I sighed heavily. "Will you at least spend the night with me again?"

"Yeah, if we can do homework. I got a speech I have to write for my Public Speaking class." Marcus set down his book bag and pulled his laptop out of it.

"For sure. I have a math test that I need to study for." I could sense that something was just not right between us and I figured it was the fact that he was hesitant to fuck me again. Deciding to brainstorm on how I could make that happen, I opened my math book, sat on the edge of my chair, and started to work through the problems at my desk. Marcus sat down on the couch, propped his feet up, and put his laptop on his outstretched legs.

After forty minutes or so, he asked me if I wanted to take a break.

Looking up from my book, I answered, "Sure."

"Will you listen to my speech?"

"Can I lie on your chest while you read it?"

He grinned broadly and said, "I would like that."

Marcus turned sideways and spread his legs. I hopped right between them, ignoring the pain from my ass, and pulled off his ankle socks. He locked his hot feet around my knees and held me in place.

"This is a nice surprise." Marcus' voice rumbled through his chest causing my head to bounce slightly.

"Feels right."

I listened to his speech and gave him constructive criticism when he was done. We fixed several problem areas and I told him how impressed I was with the logic that he had used in the speech.

"You're pretty smart for a dumb jock," I finally said.

"You're pretty smart for a cocksucker," he jabbed back at me.

We both laughed and I asked, "Wanna move to the bed and watch *The Walking Dead*?"

"Sure."

We settled on the bed together and this time Marcus stripped all the way down. I loved being able to freely explore his body this time and was barely able to watch the show because of it. Marcus was insistent that we weren't going to fuck again until I was feeling better, so I was soon able to put it out of my mind and fall asleep nuzzled up against him.

I woke early in the morning and figured that Marcus was already getting ready to go to the weight room. Instead, he was on his knees beside me on the bed and I could feel the heat pouring off of him. It was dark but I could just make him out.

"Marcus?" I asked groggily.

"I'm ready, Loch, if you are sure that you are." His voice

was deep and ragged.

I instantly came awake. Marcus wanted to fuck and I had to pinch myself to make sure that I wasn't dreaming. Propping myself up on an elbow, I felt for his hot cock and found it inches from my face. It was hard as a rock and already leaking pre-cum.

Sucking my boyfriend's cock into my mouth, I ran my tongue all over his molten rod. The three-dimensional veins on his long shaft pulsed with blood as Marcus' cock hardened even more inside my hot mouth. I explored the flange where his shaft met his cock head. Dipping the tip of my tongue into his piss slit, I tasted more of his man-nectar before concentrating on sucking on the velvety textured head.

"Fuuuucccckkkkk! You are so good at that," Marcus complimented me as he pulled his throbbing member out of my hungry hole.

"Thanks. I'm inspired by your beautiful cock."

He pulled on my shoulder andpushed me flat onto my stomach. Marcus knelt on the end of the bed, used his knees to separate my legs, and then moved into the void. He fumbled for a bottle of lube that I kept in the nightstand, found it, and greased his big lap hog generously.

"Let me know if this hurts," he ordered me, right before bending my arm back onto the small of my back and sliding his cock head into my dark hole. I was so shocked that he was holding my arm in this awkward position that I barely noticed the tremendous pain that was caused by his entrance.

"You okay?" he asked carefully.

"Fuck me, Marcus." I groaned.

"You sure?" The concern in his voice destroyed me. He was the most caring of all of the men who I had ever fucked with.

The side of my head was on the pillow with my mouth smashed flat against it, but I still managed to make my desire known by saying, "I'm going to combust if you don't drive that nail all the way inside me and fuck my brains out."

Marcus chuckled and said, "Try to keep it down. I don't want your dorm mates to hate me for the rest of the year."

"Yes, sir," I groaned into the pillow. Even though Marcus probably thought that I was kidding him by using this title, I was completely in the moment with him. When he commanded me, I was absolutely his. Hell, even when he didn't command me, I was his, but my loins burned for him even more when he mastered over me.

He pushed his hips forward and his monster cock parted my flesh. I cried out softly into my pillow as the pain completely overwhelmed me. As if sensing my pain, Marcus pulled my arm back into the small of my back and tightened his grip on it as he continued to snake his long prick inside me.

Unlike an enabling parent, Marcus knew the best way to pull a bandage off was to do it quickly without hesitation. That's what he was doing now. By holding my arm pinned against the small of my lower back, he was refocusing my attention away from the pain.

Before I even knew it, Marcus was buried to the balls inside of me.

"Feels so fucking good, Loch," he grunted into the back of my head, his voice ragged and full of need.

"Your cock feels so good splitting me apart," I whispered into the pillow, just loud enough for my new partner in crime to hear.

He stopped moving suddenly and asked, "Too much?"

"Please don't stop," I whined.

"I got what you need, Loch," Marcus growled as he began to try to saw me in half.

I loved the fact that Battle was still pressing down on my body and that he was restraining my arm behind my back as he fucked. Marcus pulled out of me and then slowly pushed his length back into me. He paused at the deepest part of his thrust each time, putting pressure on my lower back. His giant cock burned a path of destruction through my ass like General Sherman rolling through Atlanta.

Oh, God! I love being fucked by this man! But I'm afraid of scaring him off. I can't let him know that he is affecting me this way. Not yet, Marcus, not yet.

Marcus increased his speed, let go of my arm, and put both palms flat on the dip in my back. He kept pressing his body weight down on me which lifted my ass further off the mattress, giving him an open target that he was destroying.

I kept my arm pinned behind my back even though he had released it because I thought it might please him and because I could feel his stomach come down on it with each thrust, sending that familiar electrical current running to my brain. It was cold in the room from the air conditioner, but Marcus' body heat was warming my skin and the physical exertion was causing me to sweat, even though I was chilly. All of these things worked to set up a strange physical sensation that was attempting to overwhelm me.

When Marcus fell over the edge of his climax, he buried his dick so far inside me that it felt like he was shooting hot spunk onto the bottom of my stomach. He hissed through his bared teeth, "Shhhiiiiitttttt!"

I had never felt so full of and so excited by someone before and the realization of it sent me over the edge as well. Pumping my load of white hot cum onto the sheets under me, I moaned into the pillow and felt my ass muscles clench even tighter around Marcus' joint.

"That's it, Loch. Grip me just like that." Marcus lowered his body on top of mine and began to undulate his hips — driving that still hard pipe of his into and out of me again.

"Fuck me," I said loudly as I was smashed down between my big-bodied boyfriend and the mattress. I loved having him on top of me. I loved having his weight overwhelm me. I loved the way he smelled like a musky sweaty man and I loved the way his cock showed me no mercy.

Marcus reached between me and the mattress and found my hard nipples that were sore from being rubbed on the cotton sheet. Using two long rough fingers, he pinched my nipples each time he slammed his hips forward, driving me further out of my mind.

"You are so tight, Loch. I don't want to hurt you, but at the same time I want nothing more than to split you wide open and mark you as mine as deep inside you as I can reach."

His words ignited my fire and I felt my face flush at the same time as my cock hardened again. "I am yours, Marcus, so mark me." My voice was so husky that I didn't even recognize it.

The sweat rolled down my back and onto Marcus' chest. His unshaven cheek was rubbing the side of my face. His fingers intertwined mine. His legs kept mine spread apart. And through it all, Marcus' thick cock continued to pound away at my tight hole. I never wanted him to stop.

CHAPTER TWENTY-TWO

When Marcus' cell phone alarm went off early in the morning, I was ready. I had woken a little earlier and was busy watching Marcus sleep beside me. He was so cute as he slept that I found it hard to keep my hands off of him. But when his alarm sounded, his hot body was fair game.

Throwing back the sheets from him, I used the remote to turn off the air conditioner with my other hand. He stirred and reached out for his phone. I was already running my hands all over his broad chest and his morning wood.

"What's up, Loch?" Marcus asked sleepily.

Laughing and tweaking his hard prick, I answered, "You are and so therefore I am."

"Oh, yeah?"

"Oh, yeah! I'm going to get mine this morning," I informed him as I climbed on top of him. Squirting lube on my palm, I slicked up his meat missile and hoped that I still had enough cum inside me from last night to make this work.

"And what exactly is that going to be?" he asked with a smirk.

"You marked my ass as yours last night and now I'm going to mark your cock as mine." I didn't say anything else as I placed his gloriously large cock head against my puckered hole and then pushed it through. I let my body weight push me further and further down onto his big prong until it felt like I was nothing more than a flesh costume for Marcus' cock to put on.

His warm hands on my sides and our electric connection

brought me back to earth. Opening my eyes, I realized that having his cock buried to the hilt inside me caused every nerve ending in my body to fire. The pleasure center of my brain was working overtime to produce the endorphins that I needed to sustain my addiction to his fucking. I looked down into his handsome face, partially hidden by his shaggy blond locks.

"You like that, do you?" Marcus asked quietly.

"Your cock is mine. My ass is yours. It's where you belong," I said in an almost sing-song chant. I quickly shook off the pleasure fog he had me in and set my teeth to go to work. Rising up onto my knees, I let my elevator rise to the top floor of his meat shaft and then free-fall plunge back to the basement. It was quiet the drop considering he was so long and the difference between empty and full was one of the most dramatic physical feelings I had ever felt.

Increasing my speed, I fucked Marcus just as dominantly as he had done me in the past. There was a look of awe on his face as I rode his prick like a horse jockey trying to win the Triple Crown. I placed my palms flat on his thick chest, leaned forward, and worked my hips up and down as he held each of my ass cheeks apart for maximum depth of thrust.

This was my fuck. This was my man. I was going to make sure he knew and from this moment forward, I would make sure everyone knew. Our connection was complete. He was a part of me and I was an equal part of him. We were not one, but two halves of an ideal.

I could feel my climax begin in my balls, which were unceremoniously squished between his hard abs and my crotch. The waves of tension rolled up my spine and fiercely washed over my brain until I felt like I was having an out-of-body experience. My prick was painfully hard, slapping repeatedly against Marcus' skin, moist with sweat. Each slap of my dick to his stomach made the electric charge that was so unique to our coupling, surge through me.

"I'm going to come, Marcus." I groaned at him as I continued to rock myself up and down on his big tool.

"I don't want it on my face," Marcus said like a true NOMAR as he put up a big hand to shield the path in front of my cock head.

I couldn't answer since I was too far gone. At this point, I was just a body composed of hard muscles and pleasure-seeking neurons. My body took over my will and mind with two main purposes—to continue impaling myself repeatedly on his hot tool and for release.

"Fuuuuuuccccckkkkkkk!" I hissed through clenched teeth as my climax reached its crescendo and centered on my cock. Hot jets of strong-smelling spunk shot out of my piss hole and hit my footballer on his hand, covering it.

"Oh, yeah, Loch. That's the shit right there." Marcus groaned as I clamped down with my ass muscles even tighter on his huge shaft. He moved his hands to my hips and held me tightly in a solid grip while he finished himself off by fucking me so hard and fast from below that my cock continued to squirt out cum with each stroke.

When Marcus came, he was unable to talk, instead resorting to a series of grunts and groans as he filled up my ass with his sweet cream. I collapsed next to him on the bed and used my hand to clean his cock of excess cum and bring it to my mouth. He let me lick my own cum off of his hand, which I did with gusto.

"How the fuck do you do that?" he asked in awe when he was finally able to breathe normally again.

"That's what you get when you are with me," I said, like I was discussing the types of coffee carried in the local Starbucks.

"Then I will be with you for a very long time," Marcus said with the same blasé attitude.

"I hope so, because I don't want to have to train another player," I told him, chuckling.

He smacked me on the ass hard with his flat hand and said, "You going to work out with me today?"

"I thought I just did." I smirked.

He narrowed his eyes and stared at me.

"Not today, Marcus, not today," I said. "But I do want you to introduce me to someone that can put me on a work out plan soon."

He nodded and shook his head in agreement. "While we are talking about our schedules, do you think we should try to map out when we will see each other?"

"You mean you are not going to sleep over every night and fuck my brains out?"

He shot me a withering glare and said, "That's all that I want to do, but we must show some restraint."

"I agree."

"I won't be able to see you on Friday nights with my games on Saturdays."

"But today is Friday," I whined.

Marcus shot me another withering look. "And I have my first game tomorrow."

"I know. I'm grateful that you spent the night with me."

"That's better, Loch." His face suddenly transfixed into a peaceful visage. "I want you to be an asset to me and not just a distraction."

"That's what you think of me . . . a distraction?"

"No, but I know how much I love fucking you and how easily I could allow myself to fall under your spell."

"*My* spell?" I asked in shock. "You are the one that has me on a leash."

"Hmmmmm! Now there is an idea," he said lustfully.

"You like that? Maybe I can pencil you in for a Sunday sometime in the future," I said, dangling the carrot.

"I'm going to take you up on that."

"Can I see you after the game at least?"

"Of course. We will have to celebrate and I want you to watch the games."

"So, Saturday after the game until Sunday?"

"Yeah. I think I should go back to my room Sunday night to get ready for the next day."

"That's not a lot of time for me to be with you." I tried to keep the hurt out of my voice, but I could still hear it.

"Don't worry, Loch, I'm going to make sure we see each other. How about we do a Wednesday night dinner and sleep over every week?"

"That would be better," I said, managing to smile.

"We will just play it by ear then."

"I could come to your dorm sometimes."

"That would be cool, but I have a roommate."

"A football player?"

"Yeah. Jordan Josey, a freshman guard."

"I'm sure he wouldn't mind if I visit every once in a while."

"Probably not. Okay, I gotta go. Wanna shower with me?" Marcus asked as he wiped his hand on my chest.

"Hell yes!" I answered him excitedly.

"No funny business. I don't want to freak out your friends."

"All right," I said, with exaggerated whining.

Within the hour, Marcus and I were clean and my room was empty except for the strong smell of sex and sweaty men. I found it hard to study with his smell in my nose and the ghost of his hard-on lingering in my ass, so I packed up my books and headed to class early. Stopping by the student store, I bought a doughnut for breakfast and a cup of coffee, feeling the soreness in my ass with each step.

Class was uneventful and throughout it, I realized that I was unable to shake the bad feeling I was left with after my talk with Marcus this morning. I wanted him to be with me at all times already. I wasn't sure how he had bewitched me so completely in this short time, but it probably had something to do with his amazing cock.

CHAPTER TWENTY-THREE

Friday afternoon, I reconnected with my dorm friends and we wound up drinking and playing cards in Bob's room for the rest of the day. We started playing Rook and then I taught them Hand and Foot, which they picked up quickly and seemed to love.

My friends asked me a lot of questions about Marcus and I answered them as honestly as possible. They teased me about not being able to sit still for long while playing cards and I teased them about how just a week ago, it was them that went to the Service tent and spent hours inside.

We made plans for the football game tomorrow and I went back to my room late that night drunk and exhausted. I jacked off thinking about Marcus and fell right to sleep. Waking up the next morning, I grabbed my phone and frowned when I didn't have any texts or messages.

I decided to text Marcus anyway.

Game day!
You up sleepy head?
Not like I was up yesterday! I missed you last night.
Thanks. I missed your sweet mouth and ass!
You'll just have to wait, big guy . . .
All right!
Good luck today.
I won't need it. I'm probably not going to play.
You will one day. I'm proud of you for being part of the team.
I'm proud of you for being part of my team.

Team Battle! Rah rah!
Is that what you are going to yell at the game?
If you would like me to . . .
No, give the seniors their due. I'll see you after?
Yes.
Good. See ya.

I felt refreshed and invigorated by our text exchange. The campus seemed to be buzzing with the excitement of today's game and there were a lot of parents, as well as visitors all over the campus. I jumped out of bed and made my way to the bathroom. Some of the frat boys on my hall were already dressed in suits and drinking.

I got cleaned up, dressed for the game in shorts and a UNC t-shirt. I met Bob, Jeremy, Brandon, and Dave on the bench outside and we headed to the Ye Olde Waffle Shoppe for brunch. Afterwards, with full stomachs, we started the long walk across campus to Kenan Stadium.

The campus was electric with excitement. Lots of students were out partying and walking with us towards the game. There were tailgaters all over the place and loads of drunk kids along with them.

We had good seats for the game and I spent most of it trying to look for number forty-four pacing the sidelines. Marcus didn't get to play, but Carolina won the game even without him. I felt sorry for him until I saw him afterwards and realized how happy he was despite not playing.

My boys and I went as far down into the tunnel under the field as security would let us. They were good enough to wait with me at the security line until Marcus exited the locker room and headed for us.

"Awesome win!" Brandon said to Marcus as he stepped past the security guards and up to our group.

"Thanks. It was a good game for us," Marcus said humbly. His golden eyes were blazing at me as he took me in with his gaze, making my mouth suddenly go very dry. He looked awesome, freshly showered with his shaggy hair still damp hanging in his face. I swallowed hard and felt an itch deep inside my ass along with a burning in my balls. I knew if I didn't stop looking at him right now that I would soon be hard as a rock and unable to walk back to my dorm.

"You coming by later?" I asked him, trying hard to keep the lusty innuendo and desperation out of my voice.

"Absolutely. There's a team dinner and then I'll meet you at your room."

"Cool," I said, trying to sound nonchalant.

My friends started to walk back up the tunnel, saying their goodbyes. Marcus leaned into me and growled, "I've never been hotter for you. I'm going to fucking rail you out again until all you can do is stay in the bed and pleasure me."

I swallowed hard. "It will be my honor, sir," I teased him. "To the victor of the game go the spoils."

"And I'm going to spoil you over and over," he said with a wink before turning back up the tunnel and leaving me. I'm sure he was completely unaware of how he had just set me on fire and left me burning for him.

We stopped at the Pine Room to eat dinner after the game. Everyone was still very excited and when we got back to the dorm, a cornhole tournament had broken out in the quad. My buddies and I sat on the benches to watch and cheer the combatants.

Later, I felt Marcus before I even saw him. Something tingled inside me and I looked up towards the corner where the quad led to South Campus. A few seconds later, he appeared. He walked with confidence, like a lion coming straight towards his prey—king of everything. My crotch responded to the electric stimulation that shot from my brain to my balls when I put it together that I was the prey.

I was perfectly fine being the prey. And if I was going to be entirely honest with myself, I craved it and wanted nothing more than to surrender to him, lay under his weight, be dominated by him, and be his in every way. It is not what I thought I would have wanted as a younger man, but it definitely was now.

Marcus took in the scene in front of the dorm, but his eyes were laser-focused on me. Some of my dorm buddies recognized him and gave him pats on the back for the game today and several others talked to him briefly as he stood in front of me in the darkening light of the day.

The cornhole tournament had progressed to the championship round and several seats beside me on the top of the bench opened up as players switched places. I was shocked when Marcus climbed up onto the bench and sat down beside me to watch.

Someone handed him a beer and I looked at Marcus like he had two heads.

"Don't stare, Loch." His voice was husky and deep, causing an immediate visceral reaction to my body. The fact that he commanded me without even cutting his eyes at me was so hot that I couldn't even think straight.

"Don't you want to go upstairs?" I blurted out.

"Of course, but not now, Loch, not now." He smirked at his cleverness, trying not to laugh.

He let out a big whoop when one of the players holed out and then put his meaty hand on my inner thigh as we watched the rest of the game. It was such a normal kind of guy thing to do and I was pleased as punch that we were together in public. I was struck by my delight at doing such a regular activity as cheering on a make-shift game between my friends with Marcus.

When the game was over, most of the guys started to filter away and Marcus said to me, "Upstairs, Loch." The sheer rawness of his voice lit my fire even more than the command.

I didn't respond verbally, but let my body take over as I opened the dorm door and climbed the steps to my room. He was walking behind me—I knew it as much by the electrical feeling I was getting from his nearness as much as the sound of his expensive tennis shoes on the stair steps.

Marcus didn't say a word as we entered my room. He locked the door and pushed me down onto the couch in a seated position. He kicked off his shoes and climbed onto the couch, standing with his feet on either side of my hips. He didn't even strip down, but instead pulled his long thick cock through his zipper and fed it directly into my hungry hole.

Is this how it's going to go again?

I opened my mouth and stretched my lips around his huge tool while still managing to smile. He was hard as steel and as hot as if he just came out of a foundry. I surprised myself by being able to take a little bit more of him into my mouth this time and he seemed very satisfied with my effort, judging from his moans. The thick veins on his shaft were bulging with pulsing blood, making him hard as a rock.

Running my hand up his torso, I felt him up through the plaid dress shirt he was wearing. Marcus put his hands behind his ass and onto his buns, using them to push his crotch forward and give me a fast, deep face fucking. He started to leak pre-cum so I slurped the thick man-candy down as fast as he leaked it.

"Mmmmmm." I moaned as he stretched my lips wide and drove his big cock to the back of my throat with each thrust. My cock was hard as a rock by the time Marcus reached his climax.

Marcus growled as he pulled his long unit out of my mouth, hooked his thick thumb into the side of my mouth and pointed his cock head at the roof of my opened mouth. He stroked his wet shaft with his right hand and then he exploded—his nuts pumping his strong man goo into my open hole.

I kept my tongue under Marcus' giant cock head to catch any cum that might dribble down, swallowing constantly in order not to choke on his seed. I looked up at the man I had chosen and saw that he was staring down at me with such passion that I might have blushed if not for the fact that I was too busy licking his large cock like it was an all-day sucker.

Without a word, Marcus stepped off of the couch and pushed the coffee table away from it. He pulled me to my feet and placed my hands on the hem of his shirt.

I just happened to be really good at charades, so I grabbed the hem and lifted the plaid dress shirt off of Marcus. Taking a few seconds to admire his chest, I ran my hand lightly over the smooth skin of his stomach and then the hairy skin of his upper chest. The electrical current running between us was so intense that I actually twisted one of my hands to see if there was some kind of spark that I could see occurring. There was something there, but not that I could see, so I unbuttoned his shorts and pushed them with his underwear to the floor after untangling his junk from the lot.

Marcus returned my feather-light touch as he undressed me and ran his hand softly over my ass cheeks, sending exciting sparks of desire coursing through my body. Suddenly, he smacked my bottom hard with his over-sized flat hand, causing my whole body to tense up as the heat bloomed on my skin.

My footballer grinned at me as he lay down on the couch and spread his legs. I recognized the position instantly. Grabbing the tube of lube next to the bed, I gingerly sat down on the couch and Marcus' feet were soon in my lap. Noticing that he still had on his black athletic socks, I peeled them off of his gorgeous feet and rubbed the soft pads on the bottoms of his tired dogs.

"You might be the most amazing person I have ever met," he told me huskily.

"I'm not sure that I deserve your praise when all I'm doing is worshipping at the Marcus Battle flesh altar."

He laughed out loud and repeated the phrase *flesh altar.* Taking the lube from the top of the couch where I had placed it, Marcus jacked his cock with it as I finished rubbing his feet. Marcus pulled his feet off me and bent his knees.

I turned sideways and folded my legs underneath me before I leaned forward, fully exposing my ass to him. Turning my head back to look at him, I wondered if he would lube me like I needed.

A look of confusion crossed Marcus' face before it cleared and he understood what I wanted. Squirting lube on two of his fingers, he roughly pushed them inside my puckered hole. He used a twisting, thrusting motion to slick me up, making me hot as hell and craving his cock inside me more than I had ever wanted anything.

Pulling his thick fingers out of my tight hole, Marcus pulled me back towards him, wrapped me in his arms and legs, and snaked his bloated cock right into my hole. I groaned as he pushed my hips down towards his crotch, further impaling me on his big rod. He was soon buried to the balls inside of me and his throbbing monster felt bigger than it had any right to be.

This was our position and as I lay my head and back onto his massive chest, I sighed with pure pleasure. There was nowhere else I wanted to be, but lying on Marcus and feeling his huge cock punching up into my guts. There was no one else that I wanted to be with, except for Marcus Battle. I wanted him to hold me steady with his muscled arms as I lay on top of him forever.

As if he could read my mind and agreed with me, Marcus sighed underneath me.

CHAPTER TWENTY-FOUR

Marcus put on quite the show of fucking after that first football game of the season. He fucked me hard three more times before his cock decided to take a break. We lay in bed, sweaty and exhausted. Everywhere I looked in my small dorm room, I saw a wall or piece of furniture that evoked a fond memory of being pushed up against it or bent over it.

"Fuck! Is that how it's going to be after each win?" I asked in a raspy voice as I reached for a bottle of water on the nightstand.

"Oh, did we win?" Marcus acted innocent.

I returned his innocent tone, saying, "I don't know about you, but I sure won something."

"I feel like I won you," Marcus admitted.

"I am yours," I stated flatly to reassure him.

"I like hearing that," he said, growling, and pushed my head towards his crotch again. I licked and cleaned his dirty dick until it was hard and ready to go again. I was constantly amazed at his stamina and his recovery time was almost non-existent.

"How would you like me this time, my Tarheel footballer boyfriend?" I teased him.

"You pick. I just love being in that tight ass of yours."

"Doggy style in front of the closet mirror where I can watch you tearing me up," I answered quickly.

"Somebody's thought about that before," he said, chuckling.

"Just a little," I admitted with a shrug of my shoulders.

I opened the closet door and angled it towards the couch. Crawling onto the couch on all fours, I moved to the end and put my hands up on the armrest. Marcus joined me. He folded one leg onto the seat cushion and stood on the floor with the other. He gently pushed his big cock head into my rosebud.

Even though we had just done this several times in the last two hours, Marcus' huge cock parting my anal ring and sliding inside of me took my breath away each time. It always felt like he was going to tear my asshole as it stretched to its limit around him and it always felt like that giant snake would not fit inside me. However, when he was finally buried to the balls and his cock was throbbing and pounding with blood and my ass hole was burning and squeezing the shit out of him, everything was okay. It was better than okay, it was phenomenal and I couldn't get enough of it.

Watching Marcus in the mirror, I saw a look of ecstasy cross his face as he pumped his cock to the bottom of my ass. "Is that where you like to be, Marcus?"

"Every minute of every day, if I could be . . ."

"We could work something out," I said, laughing.

"I'm going to fucking tear you up now."

"Fuck me hard, Battle!" I demanded.

The image in the mirror dominated my sore ass. It was like watching my own personal porno with Marcus as the bigger athlete who discovers a love of a tight ass and can't get enough of it. I was lost in the fantasy of it as he rocked my hips back and forth, moving my ass over his hard shaft repeatedly.

Marcus huffed and puffed as he plowed a wide furrow through my dark channel. He was magnificent, like a Greek god from one of my mythology books that I'd had as a child. I could see him as Zeus, fucking me with his thunderbolt from on high or Poseidon with his wet hair spearing me with his trident. I was a mere mortal compared to Marcus, but I tried to keep his interest by using my ass muscles to squeeze his mighty scepter even more than I usually did.

"Holy fuck!" Marcus salivated at the tighter hole he had to thrust into suddenly and rewarded me for it by punching into me harder and faster. His legs started to shake as he approached his eruption.

I watched in fascination as the Greek god dominated and destroyed me. Marcus buried deep inside my ass, leaned forward over my back, reached around me and held me in a tight hug as the tension in his cock released. He flooded my anal channel with his hot fluid.

Flattening me to the couch cushions, Marcus pressed his weight down on me and breathed heavily into the side of my face. After a few beats, he said in a husky voice, "I've never felt the way I do when I'm fucking you. I didn't even know it was possible to feel pleasure like this."

"I feel the same way," I said as I reveled under his weight.

Marcus and I spent Sunday in my dorm room, me because my ass was so sore that I couldn't even walk and Marcus because he couldn't keep his cock out of my mouth and ass. Marcus cooked me Kraft macaroni and cheese for dinner while I showered and tried to scrape all his cum off and out of me. He then worked hard to fill me right back up with it.

"I love our Sundays," he finally said, too exhausted to continue.

And so our weeks went. I missed Marcus terribly when he wasn't with me, but we began to surprise each other on our off days. I would meet him outside one of his classrooms and would give him a quick blowjob in the bathroom stall or he would be waiting for me after class on the bench at my dorm and we would fuck hard and fast before he departed again for his dorm.

I lived for those small moments. The football team was

playing well and I followed all of their away games on TV and attended all of the home games. Marcus would get to play sometimes at the end of games for a play or two if the victory or loss was already decided, and I was always so happy for him in those moments.

I had begun to work out with the trainer that Marcus had recommended. His name was Burns and he was a hot piece of man. Burns was in his forties with blond hair that was always shaved into a buzz cut. He wore tight polo shirts and his huge biceps would barely be contained in the sleeves of those shirts. Sweat pants and tennis shoes comprised the rest of his uniform. Burns had a huge tribal tattoo around one bicep that extended under his shirt and a nest of dark blond hair that sprang out of the collar.

Sometimes, if Marcus and I hadn't seen each other for a couple of days, I found Burns really hard to resist. He was a lot older than Marcus and I, but he definitely had a ton of sexual magnetism left, at least for me.

One Wednesday afternoon, I headed to the weight room to meet Burns and I found him finishing up with another client. He was uncharacteristically in shorts today and I openly stared at his muscular hairy legs. But what really caught my attention today was the huge basket that was showing through his silky workout shorts.

Burns waved to me and pointed at one of the stationary bikes. I hopped on and started to pedal. He finished up with his client and walked over to me.

"What's shaking?" he asked.

"Not much," I said dully.

"Battle away with the team?" Burns knew all about Marcus and me, including the story of the football player draft and how I had picked him.

"They leave today for Miami," I answered, my voice colored with disappointment.

"Big game," Burns said, smiling.

"Yes. I hope they crush the Canes."

He looked at me sideways for a second while he increased the tension on the pedals. "But you haven't had much time with Battle this week. And he probably won't be home until Sunday night."

"Exactly," I said, wondering if Burns was a mind reader in addition to a trainer.

"I bet Battle realizes that."

"Probably. He's really good at being able to empathize."

"He probably wouldn't mind if you were able to . . ." Burns let the end of the sentence trail off and I saw a sudden flush cross his light skin.

"Able to what, Burns?" I challenged him.

"Battle probably would want you . . . provided for," he said in a rush.

I had experienced enough NOMARs trying to get into my pants in my short life to know a pick-up line when I heard one, and Burns was trying his best. I'm not sure whether it was the fact that I hadn't seen Marcus for a while or the fact that Burns was so hot, but I decided to flirt a little with him.

"And you would be able to provide for me, Burns?"

He flushed fully bright red now and replied, "I could give you what you need, Loch." Quite inelegantly, he grabbed his crotch and kneaded his big cock with the palm of his hand.

"And how do you know what I need, Burns?"

"Some of the players have told me," he stumbled over his words.

"Told you what?" I wasn't going to let him off the hook this easily.

He blushed deeply on every surface of his skin and he shifted his weight back and forth from one foot to the next. Finally, he looked up into my eyes and said, "They say that you need a big cock inside you."

"Do they?" I smirked at him.

"They do," he admitted, having the good manners to look down. He knew that it was shameful to have talked about me this way, but his desire to fuck me overruled all of his good sense and manners.

"They are partially correct," I said blandly.

He quickly looked up at me. "How can they be partially correct? You either need a big cock inside of you or not."

I laughed at his attempt at logic.

"What?"

"They are partially correct because I like a big cock inside me," I told him. "But they are wrong that I need it and they are wrong that it will be just any big cock."

My subconscious immediately sent a series of questions into my awareness. Really? Are you sure that you don't need it? Wouldn't any big cock work to scratch my itch? Don't those football players know me better than I know myself?

Burns looked at me, tilted his head and then said, "Battle thinks you need it . . ."

I stopped pedaling and spit, "What?"

The trainer reached in his pocket and pulled out his cell phone. He typed in his security code and scrolled through his texts. Finding what he needed, Burns handed his phone to me.

It was a text string from Marcus Battle.

Burns, can you do me a favor while I'm away this week?
Sure, Battle. What you need?
Take care of Loch for me?
Easy!
No, I mean . . . take care of him.
Wow! You mean fuck him?
I'll be gone for a while and Loch needs a big hard cock to keep him even. He likes you, so I think he would enjoy fucking around with you.

Loch won't cheat on you. I know that much about him.
Loch will do it if he knows that it pleases me.
You'll have to tell him to do it.
I'm not his Master. I don't tell Loch to do things.
He won't believe me.
Show him this text — Loch, the choice is yours. I would like you
to fuck around with Burns while I am gone so you don't miss me so
much. It will make me feel better about leaving you. If you decide
not to, I will be okay with that as well.

I finished reading the string and looked up at Burns. He was polite enough not to gloat.

"So, we're a go?" Burns asked a little too quickly when he saw that I wasn't going to say anything.

"Maybe. Let's see how this work out goes . . ." I said, raising an eyebrow.

"You want me to be easy on you?" he asked, digging for a solution.

"Would Marcus want you to be easy on me?"

"Fuck, no! I'm going to work you like an overweight contestant on *The Biggest Loser*."

I'm going to give you a work out like you've never had before . . . I thought to myself as I started to pedal again.

CHAPTER TWENTY-FIVE

I called Marcus during the one break that Burns gave me during the workout. Sweating up a storm, I worried about ruining my phone, but needed to hear from him.

As soon as he answered, I spit out, "Do you really want me to do this?"

"Yes," he answered. "I would feel better about leaving you and I would relax knowing that you were okay. And I would be able to concentrate on the game."

"I thought you were the jealous type?" I asked him.

"Why do you think I picked Burns? He's old enough to be your father."

I laughed and felt better about it for the first time. "Miss you. Play well."

"So, you're going to do it?"

"I aim to please you, Marcus Battle," I answered flirtatiously.

"Well, then, you play well also, Loch."

"Bye." I pressed the button to release the call and instantly smiled. I had never thought about Marcus sharing me before, but I knew that it was something that was routinely done in The Service.

I had delayed my entry into The Service in order to go to Carolina. I was one of those guys that knew exactly where I wanted to go and what I wanted to study years before arriving on campus. Realizing at some point in high school that my decision to go to college instead of into The Service would probably cost me the chance to have the same opportunity as other marked guys, I came to terms with that.

I knew what I was giving up—the chance to make millions of dollars very quickly, the chance to experience The Service, the chance to meet a NOMAR who would be my Master, and a chance at a huge sexual adventure. Telling myself that I was getting just as much in return, I thought of Marcus, my friends at school, the aching desire I had to be part of the college experience, as well as a good education.

Marcus' decision to share me, which he obviously saw as a way to provide for me, made me think of The Service. I knew from rumors that Masters routinely shared their Servants with their family members, their friends, their colleagues, and in some cases, to men from which the Master could garner advantages or favors.

Happy that Marcus had left the final decision up to me, I marveled at his restraint. Most college freshmen would not have the will to resist demeaning me, whether on purpose or not, to their friends. I could just imagine the cocky Calvin, if I would have chosen him. He probably would have me fucked by his buddies non-stop when he wasn't around. If he ever got a Servant for real, he would probably have him tied down to a bed for two years.

I was lucky to have Marcus Battle for a boyfriend and I planned to let him know it as soon as he returned. Now I needed to turn my focus back to the gym and to the salivating Burns. The outline of his big cock in his shorts got bigger and bigger as we got closer and closer to the end of my workout.

True to his word, Burns had worked me out harder than ever before. I was completely wet and limp by the time he blew his whistle, which signaled me to stop running on the treadmill.

Burns threw me a towel and asked, "How was that?"

"That was awful," I said, gulping air in between words.

Burns had been lifting weights between sessions of bossing

me around, so his enormous biceps glistened with sweat at his sides. His polo shirt and shorts were completely soaked through, as were my clothes.

The trainer laughed and said, "You did really well today. I can tell Battle that you didn't slack off one little bit and that your stamina and power is much better than when we first started."

"You gonna give a report to Marcus about me, Burns?"

"Absolutely," he said, grinning. "That kid wants to know everything about your workouts."

"Everything?" I asked with a raise of my eyebrow. "You gonna tell him about the workout we are about to do?"

"Won't you?" he challenged.

I laughed. "I'm just playing with you, Burns. Of course I will tell him, if he wants to know."

"Okay," he said with more than a hint of uncertainty. I continued to keep him off balance and he didn't seem to know what move to make next. "I'll let you get cleaned up and then maybe we can go out later?"

"We can go out later if you want to Burns, but I'm going to suck your cock and ride it while we are both soaking wet with sweat." I said it like I was telling my trainer that I liked the rowing machine more than the elliptical.

"We . . ." He stumbled. "We what?"

"We're going to go fuck, Burns," I said, grabbing him by the shoulders and pushing him towards the locker rooms.

"Wh-wh-where?" he stuttered.

"Is there a sauna?"

"Steambox?"

"Yeah. I want you all hot and bothered, Burns."

"Already am," he said, chuckling and leading me to the steambox. It was a pretty large room with two rows of wooden benches for guys to lounge on and a central hot box full of stones. A bucket of water and a Carolina blue ladle was located beside the stones.

"This will do." I smiled as I shucked off my wet clothes and dropped them on the floor right outside the door to serve as a signal to others that we were naked.

Burns just stared, his handsome square jaw hanging open. I gave him a good view of my ass before I stepped towards him and put a finger under his chin, feeling the stubbly facial hair. I pulled my finger up, effectively closing his mouth before I stepped across the vacuum-sealed doorway and into the box.

Once the door shut behind me, it seemed to jar Burns out of his stupor and I heard him quickly pulling his clothes off. I poured some water onto the hot coals and watched it instantly turn to steam. Burns appeared out of the steam in all of his naked glory.

Burns was thick and muscled with a hairy chest of blond hairs. His biceps looked even bigger outside of his shirt and his thick forearms contained bulging veins down to his rough hands. The steam parted as he walked and I got the first glimpse of his manhood.

It was hard as a rock and pointed straight up, due north, just like a compass needle. He was long with a wide girth that reminded me of Marcus, but I could see that he was not quite as large as my boyfriend. But Burns was big enough to give me pause. I licked my lips when I looked back up to him.

"Have a seat, Burns," I commanded.

He did and I bent over, sucking his plump cock head into my mouth. He tasted delicious and salty, like licking the salt off of a soft Bavarian pretzel. I put my palm flat onto his ripped chest and pushed him back onto the bench. Engulfing even more of his meat-sickle into my mouth, I kept pushing him away as I sucked in long pulling draws.

Stroking the trainer's big full balls, I noticed that they were completely covered in the same long blond hairs that were on his chest. Sucking his cock into the back of my throat, I buried my nose in his heavy bush of pubic hair, smelling his masculine musk. Sweat was rolling down every inch of my skin as I pumped my mouth up and down on his steely shaft.

"Fuck! Is this what Battle gets every day?" Burns asked with his head back.

I pulled off of him, reached up to his thick neck, and tilted his head down to look at me. "Several times a day, Burns."

"Lucky man." He moaned.

"You seem pretty lucky to me, Burns," I remarked as I stood up and straddled his lap. Kneeling on either side of his legs, I sat down onto his crotch and felt the wonderful sensation of two sweaty bodies sliding together. His big cock slid lengthwise between my buns like a Ballpark frank.

"I'll say."

"Quiet!" I ordered him, hooking my thumb into the side of his mouth and using my other hand to cover his face. Moving up and down against his big hot cock, I could feel his pulse quicken as I teased him.

Burns looked shocked at my dominance over him at first, but seemed to quickly come to terms with it. Most NOMARs considered themselves to be potential Masters who would dominate their marked Servants. In my heart, I knew that I was capable of being a Master and of dominating someone else. I practically had dominated most, if not all of my boyfriends—until Marcus Battle came along.

Marcus was different. He was a man who could say no to me. He was the kind of man who had a plan and stuck to it. Seemingly immune to my charms, I soon realized that Marcus was affected by me, but he had the fortitude to do what he thought was best. He could command and dominate me like no one else I had ever encountered. I was enamored with my new found boyfriend and missed him terribly.

Lifting myself off of Burns' lap, I maneuvered his fat cock

head onto my puckered hole before pushing myself down on him. Normally I would need lube to handle his size, but Burns' meat had so much sweat and saliva on it that it allowed me to be able to impale myself without too much pain. His wet phallus slid smoothly into my sweaty asshole, scratching an itch deep inside me that I didn't even realize that I had. But, Marcus had known. That's why he had asked Burns to fuck me.

Burns' big baby-maker punched my prostate, sending waves of pleasure running right to my brain before I settled into his lap. His wild bush tickled my ass and I could only imagine what it would feel like if he wasn't soaking wet.

My personal trainer's big prong inside me felt like I was riding on the horn of a giant saddle. Arching my back, I removed my thumb from his mouth and started to pump my body up and down like the saddle was attached to a wild bronco bull.

Burns might have had the body of a man in his twenties, but he had the experience of a man twice that old. He knew how to fuck and even though I was the one in charge, Burns fucked with style and force. It wasn't long before he had filled me with his sweet cream and then thrown me down on the wooden bench to rail me out again.

I left the gym with a sore ass and a heavy heart. I had liked riding Burns' big dong, but had fantasized about Marcus most of the time. Now though, I felt like I had cheated on Marcus in some way. I was way relaxed, but thought that I had enjoyed it a little too much. My emotions were still warring with themselves when Marcus called.

"Hey," I answered.

"Hey, Loch. Still like me?"

I snorted. "Yes, of course."

"You're not on Burns' team now?"

I could tell from his voice that he was kidding, but I could hear the underlying concern. "No way. I liked Burns, but he is no Marcus Battle."

"So you miss me?"

"Absolutely, but more importantly, are you missing me, Marcus?"

"Absolutely." He sighed over the phone. "I miss that sweet mouth more than anything."

"More than my ass?" I questioned him.

He paused and I hated that I couldn't see his face. "It's so hard to choose. I bet your sweet little ass is sore right now."

"A little, but nothing like a night with you, stud," I said, starting to laugh.

"Mmmm," he growled. "I'm going to be in that tight little chute as soon as I get home."

"I'll leave the door unlocked for you," I said lustfully.

"Don't you dare," he hissed. "If I get to your place and find the door unlocked, you will be punished."

"Mmmm." Now, it was my time to growl.

"Promise me," he commanded, his voice husky and compelling.

"I promise, sir."

"I like that," he quickly said. "Besides, if I really want to open your door, I seem to always have the key."

I chuckled, feeling free suddenly. "Yes, you do. That big key seems to fit me just right."

"We'll make sure it still fits when I get back."

"Yes, sir. We might have to try multiple times to make sure that it really fits all the way inside."

Marcus growled like a bear on the other end of the phone. "It might take all night and most of the next day," he hypothesized.

"Don't think about it, Battle. You've got a big game to play."

"A big game to watch . . ."

"Hang in there. You will get your turn," I encouraged him.

"I know. It's just hard."

"You're always hard, Marcus." I jabbed at him. Turning more serious, I informed him, "You can definitely put in your time and persevere. You are going to be great one day."

"You are always my biggest supporter. Thanks for that."

"No problem."

"No, I mean it. I feel like you are on my team."

"I am on your team. Now, go get 'em and make me proud!"

"Yes, sir," he teased me as he disconnected the connection.

Chapter Twenty-six

So, our freshman year went by very fast in this manner. Marcus and I almost never had a disagreement. We seemed to always be on the same page about most topics. Football season lasted through December and then we enjoyed going to the UNC basketball games during the winter.

Marcus was becoming fast friends with my own clique of buds and I had slept over at his dorm room after each of the home basketball games, since he lived right beside the Smith Center. I had met his roommate and teammate, Jordan, and immediately liked him.

When Marcus asked me if I would like to join him and some friends from the team for Spring Break, I jumped at the chance. Marcus informed me that his friend, Vance, was from Georgia, but his parent owned a beach house in Fort Lauderdale. He had invited Jordan and Marcus to go with him and Marcus had asked him if I could come also.

We talked about the trip and planned for the next two weeks. Marcus and I both had a lot of papers and presentations to do for our classes before we could leave, so we had spent very little time together alone.

Vance and the boys picked me up from the road behind my dorm as soon as my last class was over. Vance drove a huge white Range Rover with all of the bells and whistles. It was obvious that his family was wealthy.

The first time I met Vance was when he got out of the driver's seat and helped me throw my bag into the back of the SUV. He was a bald redhead with pale skin covered with freckles, big biceps, a square jaw, ice blue eyes, and a broad chest. Physically, he was not what I was expecting of someone who was from the south and owned a beach house, but he seemed fun-loving and carefree which did fit nicely with a beach attitude.

"Hi, I'm Vance," he introduced himself to me with his hand held out.

"Loch," I said, shaking his hand.

"So, you are the one that has taken Marcus away from us so often this year."

"Sorry about that," I said, shrugging my shoulders. Marcus appeared at the back of the car and gave me a hug.

"Cool your jets, you two. It's a long drive to Florida," Vance snarked.

"It's a big backseat," Marcus said, grinning.

"Don't you dare!" Vance threatened.

We climbed into the car and I said hello to Jordan. We got to know each other pretty quickly. Vance insisted on paying for all the gas, so the rest of us bought all the snacks and food every time we stopped. Marcus and I had promised to keep our hands off of each other, but it was really hard, just like we were. I forced him to always sit in the front while I was in the back and vice-versa so that I could control myself.

The trip down to Florida was a lot of fun and seemed to go by quickly as we talked about our exams, the football team, and the NCAA basketball tournament that had just finished. When we pulled into the driveway of the house in Fort Lauderdale, it was dark, but I could tell that the house was huge and beautiful.

"Wow, Vance, its spectacular," Marcus said in awe.

"We each get our own room," Vance said, grabbing his bag and running up the long flight of stairs to the front door. Soft lamps glowed in each room and the house was absolutely spotless. "The cleaning service was just here," Vance explained.

The three of us followed Vance upstairs to a long hallway of bedrooms. "This is your room Jordan," he said, pointing at the first door. "This one is mine," he said, pointing at the second door." His finger moved to the door at the end of the hallway and said, "That's your room, Loch, and the one beside it is for Marcus."

Marcus looked at me and then gave Vance a withering look.

Both Jordan and Vance burst out laughing. Vance quickly said, "Okay, okay, you two can have the Master suite downstairs."

"Appropriate . . ." I smirked, staring at Marcus.

"Don't make me punish you," Marcus snarled.

"Sounds like it's getting heavy up in here," Vance said. "I'm going to crash. If you guys need anything let me know . . . in the morning."

"I'm gone, too," Jordan said with a yawn as he disappeared into his room.

Marcus headed for the stairs saying, "Peace out."

"Goodnight, guys!" I called as I headed back down the stairs behind Marcus. I felt like I might explode. The sexual tension between Marcus and I was almost more than I could take. We had been so close to each other for almost a whole day without any relief. I hoped that we wouldn't hurt each other, but at the same time I hoped he fucking pounded me into next week.

Marcus went straight into silent mode, bending me over the dresser right inside the door. I would have laughed out loud in joy, but I did not want to spoil the moment. I had conveniently stashed a small bottle of lube in my shorts pockets, thinking that we might fuck at one of the rest stops, so I pulled it out now as I shoved my shorts to the floor.

My pent-up boyfriend snatched the lube bottle from my

hand and poured it onto his flaming sword. I'm not sure Marcus even rubbed it into his giant prick before pushing it inside of me. He entered me with such force and speed that it took my breath away.

I held myself slightly off of the surface of the dresser, but I lay my face down onto the smooth wood to try to anchor it in place. Once Marcus had his sword buried to the hilt inside of me, he let out a huge sigh and ran his large hand up my spine.

I knew this was his way of checking to see if I was okay, so I reached back with my hand and gave his furry ass cheek a squeeze to let him know that I was good-to-go. We had perfected this silent communication over the last year.

It was all Marcus needed to know. He pulled his big cock out of me, causing his mushroom-capped cock head to prod my prostate in the process. This sent waves of purple-hued passionate energy running throughout my body. He slammed back into me as hard and deep as he ever had and then proceeded to fuck me fast as we both reached our climaxes within seconds of each other.

My cock was sandwiched between the dresser and the weight of my body as it erupted, sending a torrent of hot cum onto the top of the dresser.

"Fuuuccckkkk!" Marcus moaned. "How are you so fucking tight?"

A brief panic ran through me as I asked, "Is it too tight for you?"

"Hell, no! It can never be too tight," he said into the back of my head as he draped his body over mine. "I'm just constantly amazed at how you can take my cock and then bounce right back and be so tight again."

I laughed. "I feel the same way about you, Marcus. You fuck me so hard and totally make me your cum bucket, but then within seconds you are ready to go again. How do you do that?"

"I'm inspired by you," he said as he wiggled his hand under my belly, lifting me off of the dresser and onto the bed. "Speaking of being ready to go again . . ." He growled, which soon turned into a chuckle.

"See what I mean?" I asked, laughing into the comforter on the bed.

Marcus grabbed each one of my feet and held them like reigns to a chariot as he knelt between my wide-spread legs and pushed his thick horse whip into me over and over again. He was meant for greatness—a modern day charioteer, a Roman god riding in the middle of the Coliseum to the cheers of the roaring crowds.

I felt like I was in an adult version of a wheelbarrow race. The harder Marcus thrust the more he pulled up on my legs. It was a unique position and I moaned my approval to him and he grunted his delight back to me.

Collapsing on top of me again, Marcus pumped me full of more hot semen as he gasped for breath and jerked through his climax. I loved this position with his sweaty chest plastered to my back, his mouth so close to my ear, and his weight bearing down on me. It was almost as good as when he was dominating over me, but in a much more intimate way.

Marcus and I barely got any sleep that night. Telling ourselves that we were making up for lost time we fucked constantly, not being able to get enough of each other. It was a great start to the vacation.

That week, Vance and Jordan went to several of the local events that they had for the Spring Breakers, returning to the house and telling us wild stories of the raves and parties that usually involved multiple Service Station employees hired for the event. Marcus and I were content to hang with each other, but Vance and Jordan insisted that we go to a party on the beach the last day before we left, right down from our house.

The four of us spent the day on the beach together and came inside to get cleaned up for the party in the afternoon. It wasn't like we were going to wear anything special, but I didn't want to go to a party with sunscreen and sand all over me, so I showered and put on a new pair of board shorts and a tight t-shirt. Marcus looked good enough to eat in a pair of floral print swimming trunks and a white wife-beater that showed off his tan. He was one of those rare people who could tan regardless of his blondish coppery hair.

The four of us sat down in front of the TV and ate BLT sandwiches and chips while we watched part of NBC's Olympic coverage. We ate fast and were soon ready to go. Deciding on walking, we made a formidable quartet as we approached the party.

The party was basically a section of the beach that had been cordoned off with temporary walls. There were several bars on each side of a central huge stage decorated with inflatable palm trees and ocean animals—very Spring Break spectacular.

Security at the door was tight so we waited in line for at least ten minutes before getting up to the guard. Signs everywhere said that you couldn't get in unless you were eighteen, and that alcohol would never be served to anyone under twenty-one years old.

The security guard, whose nametag proclaimed him to be Deci, was a huge black guy in his twenties. He was overweight, but had the type of build and body that told anyone not to think that was going to stop him from beating their ass.

We held up our IDs and his eyes went right to my mark, as almost everyone's eyes did. He looked from the electric blue of my jawline right up into Marcus' face.

"You got him?" Deci asked in a deep southern drawl, still looking at Marcus.

"I got him," Marcus said firmly.

Deci smiled, revealing a mouthful of crooked teeth. "I

started to say, man. He's going to get eaten alive in here."

"I can handle myself," I told him defiantly.

"Not in here with these hooligans," Deci said matter-of-factly. "It's a good thing you brought your security detail," he said looking from Vance to Jordan and back to Marcus.

"I like you," Marcus told the guard while he beamed at him.

"Because he recognized you as my protector?" I asked, my words dripping with sarcasm.

"Well, yeah," Marcus said, beaming down to me.

"Thanks for the warning, Deci," I said, pushing through the throng of guys at the gate in order to gain entrance. My three friends quickly fought through trying to keep up with me.

"I need a drink," I said to them, once they had caught up. There were hundreds of guys packed into the small space and most of them were shirtless and shoeless in the sand. It was like a huge meat buffet for my eyes, even though almost none of them held a candle to Marcus Battle.

"The bar is over here!" Vance yelled over the deafening music from giant speakers on the stage and the sound of hundreds of guys talking and laughing loudly.

We followed Vance over and he ordered bottles of beers for us.

"I thought it said they wouldn't serve alcohol to minors," I quickly said.

The bartender looked at me for the first time and I watched as his eyes flicked over my mark and then back to my eyes. He licked his lips suggestively and answered, "Those signs are just for the police so we don't get shut down. If you got the cash, we will sell to you."

"Lovely," I said under my breath. The bartender, while not bad-looking, reminded me of one of those people who are still trying to live their glory days long after they were over. His greasy-looking black hair was just a tad too long and the multiple tattoos on his muscled arms and chest looked random and desperate.

He handed us the bottles and four shot glasses full of a swirling blue liquid. "On the house. They match your mark," he said with an unnecessary point of a dirty finger.

We thanked him and turned to look for a less crowded spot. The four of us were getting a lot of attention. Marcus, Jordan, and Vance were huge football player types, but, even though I could probably pass for a football player, I was the center of most of the attention thanks to the thick blue line going from my ear to my chin.

Vance led us to a spot near the port-a-potties that had a wooden bar to put our beers on. It was a good spot to people watch. Jordan and Marcus had to stop two drunk guys from falling over me in their enthusiasm to talk to me. They downed their shots afterwards as they high-fived each other.

"What is it?" I asked Marcus afterwards.

"Dunno. Something tropical."

Jordan chimed in with, "Tastes like pineapple."

I made a *what-the-hell* face and held up my shot before downing it. Vance sucked on his beer and watched my face to see my reaction before he touched his. It wasn't half bad, but my body shivered with the strength of it.

Turning my back to my buds, I watched as a band took the stage and started getting ready to play. Marcus soon guided my back to his chest and wrapped his arms around me in a definite signal for the other NOMARs to stay the fuck away from me.

It was very hot and I was starting to sweat like a pig by the time the band started playing. My shirt was soaked through in the back. I looked down and saw that Marcus' arms were drenched in sweat as well. Pushing forward so that I could get off of him and give him some air, I stumbled forward and felt a sharp bolt of pain in my head.

Whipping around in confusion, I looked at Marcus and saw that he had fallen to the sand under the wooden post. His eyes were open, but he looked completely dazed. As if in slow motion, I scanned to the other side and saw that Jordan's eyes were closed and he was slouched against the bar.

In a panic now, as my head throbbed harder and harder, I looked at Vance who smiled at me from two different places. I shook my head and realized that I was having double vision.

I had never taken a class at The Service Academy, but my dad had taught me how to protect myself. One of the best lessons he had taught me was not to hesitate when I thought something was wrong. My father knew way before I did that the world was a hostile place for me — holding dangers that most guys never even imagined were possible. He had prepared me well, because at this moment I knew something was wrong.

Without another second of hesitation, I spun around and bolted for the front entrance. I was swaying and bumping into people — bouncing off of them like a pinball as I fought my way through the crowd. By the time I reached Deci, who was propped on his stool still letting people into the party, I had almost blacked out.

Deci caught me as I flung myself onto him with my last ounce of energy and said, "Roofie."

It was the last thing that I remember from that night.

CHAPTER TWENTY-SEVEN

I woke up the next day in a hospital bed. Marcus was sitting in a chair beside my bed looking at a magazine. Sitting up, I grabbed my head as it started to spin. I still felt like I was going to throw up.

Marcus noticed me waking and reached over to steady me. "I felt the same way when I woke up."

"How long ago?"

"Ten, fifteen minutes. We were drugged."

"Vance?" I whispered.

"He's okay. Still out. Jordan started to come out of it a minute or two before you did."

"Vance was drugged, too?" I asked, still holding my head.

Marcus looked at me and stared. "Did you think he was the one who drugged us?"

"Wasn't he?" I asked quietly.

"No. He's out cold just like the rest of us. Why did you think so?"

I told Marcus about Vance not drinking the shot and him smiling at me as I started to feel the effects of the drug. He believed that I must have just misread Vance's hesitation at doing the shot. We were soon joined by a police detective and Deci, the security guard from the party.

"Loch! How you feeling?" Deci asked when he saw that I was awake.

"My head is killing me." I was about to ask Deci what happened when the detective took over. He flung back the cloth walls on either side of me and revealed Vance in a bed to my

183

right and Jordan sitting up on a bed to my left.

"I'm Detective Rivas with the Fort Lauderdale Police Department. I understand that the four of you guys believe you were drugged at a party on the beach last night." The detective was a hot Hispanic man with dark eyes that seemed to penetrate right inside me.

"They *were* drugged," a doctor said, stepping into the cubicle. He had a clipboard and referred to it now. "They all had the same drug, Flunitrazepam, in their systems."

"Thank you, doctor." The detective turned back to us and said, "Who would like to tell me the story?" He pulled a small notebook and pen out of the inside of his jacket.

I looked at Marcus and Jordan and then shrugged my shoulders. "I can." I listed my full name, birth date, and home address for him.

"Go ahead," Rivas said to me.

"My friends and I got to the party by leaving the house we were staying in and walking down the beach. We got to the band shell right after seven. We met Deci there when he checked our IDs."

"And then?"

"The party was crowded. We went to the bar for a beer." The detective raised an eyebrow. The bartender talked to us for a minute, gave us the four beers that we ordered and also four shots that we didn't. "Oh, it was him," I said, suddenly having the fog in my brain clear somewhat.

"We've been watching those bartenders for quite some time, but have not been able to catch them. Go on."

"Some drunks tried to get at me and Marcus, and Jordan stopped them. They celebrated with the shot. I drank mine next and then I remember getting really hot. I could feel Marcus sweating profusely and when I pulled myself off of him, I was dizzy. Then I watched as Marcus collapsed onto the sand. Jordan was slouched unconscious on the bar where we had been standing."

"And Vance?"

I looked over at my new friend and saw that he was groggily trying to sit up in the bed. "Well, he was just smiling at me like nothing was wrong."

"And what happened next?"

"I took off."

"Running?"

"Yes, sir."

"Where were you running to?"

"Deci," I said, pointing at the security guard.

"Why?"

I looked at Marcus for support and his eyes urged me to tell the detective everything that I knew.

"My Dad taught me to always be suspicious of NOMARs trying to do me harm. As soon as I realized that I had been drugged, I had to get help. I knew that Deci had just seen us come in and that he would know that we weren't drunk, so I ran to him."

Rivas turned to the security guard and asked, "Did he say anything to you?"

"He said one word—roofie."

"I did?" I asked in surprise.

"You did and then you passed out," Deci answered with a smile at me.

"It probably saved you from being kidnapped or gang-raped at that party," Rivas said flatly. "Nice going."

The detective finished with several questions and then left us his card on the way out. A nurse came right in and told us we were free to go whenever we were ready. The four of us chatted excitedly about what had happened until we finally ambled out of the hospital and back to the beach house.

It had been a hell of a night and the four of us decided on the spot to extend our vacation by one more day, before collapsing exhausted into our beds. I slept like the dead and when I finally woke up the next day, I thankfully felt like myself again.

Stumbling out to the kitchen, I was drawn by the smell of bacon and coffee. Marcus was cooking all alone, so I propped myself on the door frame and said, "Now, I could get used to this."

He laughed without even looking at me. "You better?'

"Yes, you?"

"I'm good, now that I got that sleep." He handed me a mug of coffee and I sat down on the bar stool and watched him making eggs. "I think that was the first time that we have ever been in a bed together and only slept," he said with a wink.

"I can't believe that happened to us," I said by way of broaching the subject of the drugging. "And I feel so bad that I thought it was Vance."

"You weren't thinking straight," Marcus replied. "I'm the one that was the asshole, because I couldn't even protect you when you needed me to."

I could hear the hurt in his voice and it made my heart break. "There was nothing that you could have done."

"You did something," he snapped, turning around and staring at me.

I figured that he was angry at himself and not me, so I went to him and grabbed his face in both of my hands. "I have been taught since I got my mark what to do. You are a NOMAR. You aren't constantly on edge like us marked guys are. We are conditioned to look for problems and constantly process how to avoid or get out of them, if they occur."

"I know, but I feel like shit about it," he said miserably. "I promise you, Loch, that I will be there to protect you from now on. It's my job and I'm going to make sure that I protect you, if you will let me."

"Don't blame yourself, Marcus. Of course, I will let you

protect me whenever you want to." I let go of his face and went back to my coffee. "You know what I think we should do?"

"No, what?"

I smiled mischievously. "I think we need to clear that experience out of our minds by replacing it with something better."

"Is that what they taught you in those psych classes?" Marcus smirked.

I ignored him and continued, "I think we should spend the day on the beach and then have a little party of our own."

Now I had his attention. "What kind of party?"

I took a deep breath, not knowing how my boyfriend was going to take this idea of mine. "Well, if it's okay with you, why don't the four of us fuck around? Just to blow off steam and clear our heads."

"You don't mind doing that?"

"No."

"Seems like a lot of work for you."

"It's more play than work," I shrugged while I smiled at my boyfriend.

He was silent for a minute while he considered it. "I think it would definitely take the edge off and if you are willing to do it, I will support it." He said this with all the business efficiency as a judge agreeing to accept a plea of leniency from a lawyer.

"Thanks, Battle. You're the best boyfriend ever," I said, ignoring his matter-of-factness and giving him a big hug. "When can we tell the boys?"

"How about now?" Marcus said with a jerk of his head. I followed the line of his head jerk and saw Vance and Jordan standing in the hallway, smiling like crazy.

"What do you think about that, boys?"

"I think we are the luckiest stiffs to ever be drugged,"

Vance said excitedly.

"Stiff is what you better be around him," Marcus snorted as he laid the food out on the island. Everyone laughed as we dug into breakfast.

Later that afternoon, we came in from the beach, showered, and then got right to business. Marcus hadn't touched me since before the drugging, so I was more than ready to be fucked. My ass was itching from deep inside, an itch needing to be scratched. The energy amongst the four of us was off the charts.

Vance and Jordan came to the master bedroom in their towels, fresh out of the shower. I was stretched out naked on the bed, blowing Marcus when they came in. Marcus and I had already arranged this in order to avoid the awkward start that I could see coming.

Jordan immediately dropped his towel and joined us on the bed.

"Fuck, Jordan. Just barge right in," Vance said.

Jordan rumbled in his deep voice, "Christ! I've had to try to sleep in the same room while these two were fucking like bunnies all year long, so I'm entitled."

"Come here and let me repay you, you big lug," I said, before I sucked his fat prick into my hot mouth.

"Damn, that's good." Jordan moaned as I completely gorged myself on his thick cock, even though my eyes were totally on Vance as he lowered his towel to the floor. His skin was still pale and freckled, even after five days at the beach. A glorious dick, average in girth but long enough to give me pause, rose out of a nest of fiery red pubic hair.

Marcus seemed to be surprisingly comfortable with sharing me with his friends. I wasn't sure, because even though sharing a Servant with friends and even family was a common practice amongst Masters, Marcus had shown no inclination towards it at all.

Vance joined us on the bed and I used both hands to keep two cocks happy while I used my mouth on the third one. Both Vance and Jordan could not keep their traps shut during the experience. Marcus and I were used to being quiet and focusing on each other, but that wasn't going to happen with these two in the room. They complimented me on my sucking ability and talked to Marcus about how jealous they were of him being able to have *this* any time he wanted.

Vance said that his father had enjoyed a variety of Servants over the years and that he had even lost his virginity to one when he was twelve and he thought I was in the same league with the best of them.

"Wait until you get in that ass," Marcus said in a rush as he groaned loudly, grabbed my head in a big hand, and erupted in my mouth. His cum flowed like a busted sewer pipe in the street. I continued to suck and lick him clean, finally coming off of his thick pipe.

Looking up at him, I said, "Good God, someone has missed me the last two days."

"I did," he agreed, tousling my hair and putting my face onto Jordan's joint.

Jordan immediately pulled out of my mouth and said, "I don't wanna come in your mouth."

"Are you a one and done, Jordan?" I asked him.

"I am," he said, as he hung his head in shame.

"Hey," I said to him as I reached up and raised his chin so I could see his eyes. "Marcus was a one and done when I met him also."

"I was not!" Marcus said loudly. He was lying back against the pillows, glaring at me.

I burst out laughing at his face getting red. "Jordan, it doesn't matter how many times you shoot. It just takes once when you have a cannon like yours."

"Thanks, Loch," he said with a smile and a rightful nod of his head to his two friends.

"Well, I wanna come in his mouth and his ass," Vance said eagerly.

"I guess I'm a done deal then," I smirked as I went back down onto his long cock. I let him snake into the back of my throat and then he filled my mouth with scalding hot spunk. Vance's cum was more bitter than my boyfriend's and it made me wonder if it depended on what he had just eaten that would cause that bitterness.

I continued to take long drawing pulls on Vance's hose until it was exhausted. Unlike Marcus, Vance's cock shrunk after his orgasm and I was soon on all fours getting it from behind from Jordan while I sucked on my boyfriend's all-day sucker.

Marcus' roommate was pretty good at pumping my hips back and forth across his fat cock while he stayed perfectly still. His climax came quickly and without much fuss.

"Ugggghhhhh," Jordan grunted behind me.

"Fucked me good, Jordan."

"Damn, Loch! That was fucking amazing," Jordan gushed.

I chuckled, turned my head around to look at him, and asked, "You sound surprised?"

"I've seen and heard how many times Marcus fucks you in a day and look at him . . . he's got a horse cock."

"Yeah, so?" Marcus asked.

Jordan continued, "How in the hell can you take that monster so many times every day and keep your ass as tight as the one that I just fucked?"

We all burst out laughing and I answered him with, "Ours is not to question, Jordan, but to enjoy."

"Now, move over and let me show you how it is done," Vance said as he pushed Jordan who rolled onto the side of the bed. Marcus held his legs up out of the way.

Vance knelt between my legs and then pushed me to the

bed with a hand on my lower back. He kept that hand on my lower back, pushing me down, as he fed that long pale cock into me. Vance was pretty experienced fucking marked men and it showed. He fucked me long and deep.

"Trying to poke your cock up into my throat, Vance?" I smirked.

"I'm trying to give you this entire big monster, Loch," Vance groaned. "Battle, *how* is he so fucking tight on my shit? Jordan's right, it doesn't make any sense. Haven't you been dicking him for months now?"

"Don't be crass, Vance," Marcus snapped. "Loch has a special gift that I can't explain," he said, his voice softening.

"I'm tearing up that special gift," Vance hissed through clenched teeth as he buried himself into the bottom of my ass and filled me with his hot cream.

"Yeah, you are," I moaned into the mattress.

Vance recovered himself, pulled out of me, and then said, "Loch that was awesome. No wonder Battle can't leave you alone."

"He better not," I said, looking up at the man with whom I was obsessed. Vance approached my face and I cleaned his cock up for him, as well as getting it to produce some more man-cream for me.

"He's going to take his turn right now," Marcus said, his voice husky with need.

"You have been very patient, my man," I said to Marcus between licks of his friend's hot dick.

I was pretty sure that all of us had forgotten our recent trauma — at least for the moment.

CHAPTER TWENTY-EIGHT

Spring soon turned to summer and I realized that there was not much time before we left for summer break. I decided to have a talk with Marcus about what would happen over those months the next time he slept over. That talk came the weekend before finals week.

Marcus and I had just finished a particularly intense and long fuck session after going out to a dance club with my friends the night before. I had experienced three orgasms during the marathon session and Marcus probably had come twice that many times. I was completely full of his sticky spunk and mostly covered with it when I snuck out of my room to shower.

Just beginning to scrub his DNA off of my skin, I looked up to see that he had woken and followed me into the showers. Marcus didn't say a word, but held out his hand for the pouf and began to scrub me clean. He was meticulous about cleaning me, like I was a prized possession. I loved his attention to me and was glad that it extended beyond the bedroom. I shampooed his shaggy head while he scrubbed me and then returned the favor to him when he was done.

When we were both clean, our cocks were at full mast from the closeness of each other. *How is this even possible? We both should be spent!* I reached down and tweaked his hardened member, watching it bounce.

Marcus smiled a half-smile and lathered up his long schlong with body wash. He looked up and indicated for me to do so as well. My old dorm had a series of pipes running through the top of the shower and one was low and narrow enough to hang from.

I looked back at Marcus and his smirk told me what he wanted me to do just as well as his words would have. He put his oversized hands on my waist and I jumped. He held me while I got my grip on the pipe and then he placed my ankles onto his broad shoulders.

Gently, he eased the huge phalange of his cock head into my sore hole, stretching my anal ring wide. Marcus kept pushing, filling me up with his hard organ until he was buried to the nuts inside of me. I felt like I had been missing something for the last hour. We had fucked so much that I didn't feel right without his cock inside me. He was truly like the missing puzzle piece that was needed to complete me.

Marcus reached up and pulled on my arms, indicating for me to release the pipe. I did and he wrapped my arms around his thick neck. Once released from the pipe, he walked us over to the tiled wall and put my back into it. Marcus pinned me to the wall with his body weight and made sure that I was secure there.

The football player from Ohio stared into my eyes as his hips worked back and forth, driving that sledgehammer into me over and over. His golden eyes were light today and the flecks of color seemed to swirl as if they were blown by an invisible wind. This man was the most intense person I had ever known and he was completely focused on me most of the time which was a little overwhelming. However, in this case with him fucking me so deeply and completely, I was grateful for it.

Marcus was the man I had always hoped to meet. And now I had him.

So, what was I so worried about? Losing him?

I saw how much it hurt him on spring break when he couldn't protect me and I knew how much he cared about me.

Couldn't he be relied on to go a summer without forgetting

me? Who was I kidding? He couldn't go ten minutes without being inside me. How did I expect him to go three months?

I came out of my thoughts to see that Marcus could tell that I had been somewhere else. His whole face was shadowed with concern and questions, even while his lower half continued to drive his magnificent piece of man-meat inside of me time and time again. I wanted to tell him that everything was going to be okay, but I didn't dare break the connection that we had at the moment.

Readjusting my arms around his neck, I pulled myself up tighter to him and lay my head down on his shoulder. I felt closer to him than ever before and vowed to have a conversation with him as soon as we left the bathroom.

Marcus came in a flood of scalding hot cum and I marveled at how fast his nuts could produce the stuff. He let me slide all the way down on his massive missile and held me there while he pumped me full of his man cream. His shaggy wet head hung beside mine as he breathed heavily into my shoulder. I rubbed his muscled back while he returned to me.

"We need to talk," he finally said as he lowered me to the ground.

Once again, we were on the same wavelength. I nodded my head in agreement as I cleaned us both again under the warm water of the shower. We dried off in silence and headed back to my room.

"Help me strip the bed, please?" I asked once my dorm door was locked behind us. My room smelled heavily of sweat and cum and my bed was fucking destroyed.

"Sure." I got a new sheet set out of the bottom drawer of my dresser. I had asked for three sets for Christmas from my father and seen his look of disapproval when I excitedly opened them under the tree that holiday.

Marcus and I made short work of getting the bed back into shape again. I put on some music and got us each a bottle of water. Since I had been with Marcus, I had tried to eat healthier and drink more water. He and Burns had made sure that I never missed a workout and I looked better and stronger than I ever had. Marcus also looked bigger and fitter than at the beginning of the school year, so I knew we were doing something right.

My footballer grabbed my arm by the elbow and led me over to the couch. "Ready to have that talk?"

"Yes."

"Mind if we assume our favorite position for it?"

"I can't see your face in that position."

"What do you need to see my face for?"

"Duh," I said sarcastically. "To tell what you are thinking or feeling."

"You can tell that by my cock, can't you?" Marcus sat down, turned sideways on the couch, and raised an eyebrow. Once again, he knew me better than anyone else.

"Probably," I conceded.

"C'mon." Marcus signaled for me to come to him while he held his legs apart. I was helpless to not obey him. I didn't want to disobey him anyway. Marcus' power over me gave me a sense of security that was new for me, in addition to turning me on like crazy.

I sat down between his legs and slid back onto his naked body. Marcus' cock was hot against my back, even in its softened state. Marcus wrapped his legs around me and hooked his feet under my knees. His strong arms held me in a vice grip around my chest. I sighed heavily. This was where I wanted to be.

"We need to talk about what happens after finals," I said softly.

"I know. What are your thoughts on it?" he echoed my tone of voice.

"Will I get to see you this summer?"

"Maybe."

I couldn't help but feel like my heart was breaking. There was a tightening of my chest that was very unpleasant. "I could come up to see you in Ohio."

"Or I could come down to South Carolina," he said hopefully. "Do you know what you're going to do this summer?"

"I've got a job lined up with IBM. You working for your dad?" I knew from past conversations that Marcus' father owned a construction company.

"Yes. He's got a trainer at the local college to work me out afterwards. I want you to continue to work out, even though Burns won't be there to hound you."

"Yes, sir," I said sarcastically. I was rewarded by the sudden twitching of his cock against my skin.

"I'm serious. It works for us, doesn't it?"

"It does," I had to admit. "I will continue to make you proud of me, Marcus."

"Good."

"When will you come back to campus?" I asked.

"Football camp is at the end of July and I will just stay until school starts at the end of August."

"Camp lasts for two weeks?'

"Yeah. It's two weeks of torture."

"I've heard that you guys get a lot of ass, though." The full-fledged football orgy at the end of football camp was one of the biggest campus rumors I had heard this year. It was supposed to be legendary and everyone on the team referred to it when I was around them.

"Yeah, on the weekend between the two weeks. It's legendary, if you can trust the rumors about it."

I was silent.

"You jealous?"

"Not really," I answered, even though I knew I was.

"It's just a pressure release."

"I know." I could hear the raw emotion in my voice. "Speaking of that, will you need a lot of pressure release over the summer?"

"You know me," he answered almost in a whisper.

"So, yes," I quickly said.

"I'll whack off thinking about your sweet ass a lot," he said while he chuckled and squeezed me with his arms and legs.

"And visit a Service Station?"

"Probably. What will you do?" he asked tentatively.

"I'll wait for you."

"I don't think you should."

"What?" He had thrown me for a loop. Marcus was always good at saying or doing the opposite of what I expected of him, but this one was a complete showstopper.

I heard Marcus sigh and the resignation in his words when he finally spoke again. "I think you should think about taking a lover over the break."

"Why?"

"I know you. You need a hard, deep fuck every so often. It helps you stay even and think straight. Three months is too long for you to go without," he said flatly and I knew his words to be true.

"I don't want anyone but you," I said softly.

His cock hardened noticeably under my back. "I know, but you will need to find someone. Preferably someone older, please."

"Someone older?"

"Yeah, older like Burns. I can handle the thought of it better if the guy is old."

And with that statement, Marcus admitted to me for the first time that he was jealous of anyone being with me when he could not. I smiled to myself, knowing now that we were in the same boat. We felt the same way about each other and even though we knew what each other needed, it didn't sit well with either of us.

"So, you want me to try to . . . regulate myself with an older NOMAR while we are apart?"

"I think that is for the best."

"You make it all sound so scientific."

"It's . . . it's . . . overwhelming for me, Loch. You have been the most fantastic thing that has ever happened to me and this year has been . . . unbelievable. The thought of three months without you is . . . depressing, at best. I feel like I have to tell you to do this, because it is what will get you through the summer and back to me. It's selfish of me, at best."

It was the most heartfelt I had ever heard Marcus speak. "I agree," I said as I absentmindedly stroked his muscular forearms.

"In addition, I want you to be super-safe and not go anywhere alone while you are away from me."

"Okay, overprotective," I said, chuckling.

If I could see him, I would bet that he was actually rolling his beautiful eyes at me. "I'm serious. I don't want something like Lauderdale happening again or worse."

"I know," I said, stroking his feet with my legs. "I won't put myself in jeopardy."

"If you want to pick another player next year, I will understand," he said in a rush of words. I heard him hold his breath afterwards as he waited for my response.

I snorted. "Why in hell would I want to do that?"

"I don't know, to find someone better?"

"I'm pretty sure there isn't anyone better than you."

"You haven't grown tired of me?"

"I will never get tired of you, Marcus Battle. You are stuck with me," I said with a laugh.

He let out a huge breath and said, "I'm good with that." Marcus' huge cock hardened against my back. "You saw something in me that I didn't even know was there. How did you do that? How did you know?"

"I didn't know. If you remember, I wanted to see your cock and fuck before I chose you."

"But I didn't let you." Marcus' cock pulsated with his memory of our early days. "And you picked me anyway."

"I know. It made no sense, but I just felt that it was the right thing to do. Plus, I loved that you didn't give in to me like every other NOMAR always has."

"I'm glad that it all worked out, just like it will this summer."

"You know what I would be good with?" I asked lustfully, referencing his comment from earlier.

"Does it involve one of my body parts being inside one of yours?" he asked innocently.

"Of course!"

Marcus hugged me to him tighter than ever. "I'll never get tired of hearing that!"

CHAPTER TWENTY-NINE

Marcus spoiled me during finals week by fucking my brains out each day at five o'clock. He said it was a stress reliever and I didn't disagree. I had never felt so relaxed! We walked to Franklin Street each day afterwards and discussed how our exams had gone.

Our new routine made me very happy and I let myself daydream that this could be our regular life one day. I was afraid of getting my hopes up, so I chastised myself for letting my guard down. Besides, in order for that dream to come true, Marcus would have to fall in love with me and NOMARs just didn't do that.

My year with Marcus had been really exciting and I didn't want to do anything at the end of it to ruin my opinion of it. I was constantly afraid of pressing him too far or pushing him away in some manner. I had to find a way to come to terms with it all. I couldn't live under that constant stress and vowed to reconcile my feelings and return with more confidence from the summer.

I finished my last exam on Friday morning and Marcus finished his that afternoon. My dad and brother were coming to Chapel Hill tomorrow to pick me up for summer vacation. When I made arrangements with them, I had informed them about Marcus and asked if we could drop him off at the airport on our way out of town. They had agreed and I was almost completely packed for home when Marcus knocked on my door. I knew it was him, because all of my friends had already left for the summer and I could feel my draw to him, even through the thick wooden door.

"We're ordering pizza tonight, because we're not leaving the bed," he said as he barreled into the room. I was left holding the door and laughing at him.

"You trying to put some blowjobs in the bank for the next three months?"

He smirked at me as he shucked his clothes off and said, "Just trying to be fiscally responsible."

I snorted. "I'll give you fiscally responsible."

Marcus had worn flip flops to my room and I could see that his dogs were dusty. He was soon naked on the bed, his hard cock standing at attention. I reached for a damp washcloth that I had hanging on the radiator from my last trip to the bathroom.

Kneeling beside the bed, I took his right foot into my hand and slowly began to wipe the dust from it. Making sure to get between his toes and up onto his ankles, I conducted a very thorough cleaning. I loved the smell of his feet and the almost-electrical charge that occurred when our skin touched. My cock was so painfully hard by the time I finished that I was unable to do anything else but continue with Marcus' foot regime that I had planned out in my head.

Using my thumbs, I bore down into the soft pad on the underside of his foot. Marcus was propped up on his elbows, intently watching me, but when I pressed the nerve centers on the bottom of his foot with force, he had no choice but to throw his head back and groan from deep inside his chest.

I gave my attentive boyfriend a superb foot rub—working his ankle, pulling his big square toes, and massaging his heel. But now was my time. Leaning into him, I began to suck on his instep. The taste of his skin was amazing and my tongue constantly stroked it as my lips caressed and sucked him. Moving to his heel, I gave it the same attention.

Making sure that I had his full attention, I held Marcus'

stare as I slowly gorged myself on his big toe and then quickly added the others to my mouth. I ran my tongue between each toe, making sure to get them all wet.

"Christ!" Marcus said in a rush of breath.

I smiled to myself in satisfaction, but the crowning moment was still to come. Licking from his heel to his toes, I covered the complete bottom of his right foot before moving onto his left one.

As I repeated the foot bath on Marcus' other hoof, I was rewarded with his moans of pleasure again. Soon, both of his feet were wet with my saliva and I was ready for my release. Pushing his two big feet together, I licked the bottom pads like an ice cream cone as I used my hand to jack my painfully hard dick. I was already so close to my orgasm that it didn't take more than a few strokes.

When I fell over the edge of my climax, I stood on shaky legs and bent over Marcus' feet. My piss slit opened and ropy strands of hot spunk shot out of my cock and onto my boy-friend's feet. I continued to milk cum out of my sensitive tool as Marcus looked at the scene with what looked like wonder on his face.

As soon as the waves of sensitivity subsided, I dropped back to my knees and set about cleaning up my mess. I licked every inch of Marcus' feet again, cleaning cum off with my tongue. It was a double treat for me.

"God damn," Marcus sighed when I had finished, un-dressed, and crawled onto the bed beside him. He wrapped a muscled arm around me and asked, "So, that's how you want to start our last session before break?"

"Yes, sir," I answered, teasing him.

His eyes narrowed at me, but the lust in them told me that he was so totally into me addressing him as my superior. "Then, I'm going to have to step up my game."

"You better," I said flippantly.

Marcus responded with a deep-throated growl as he pushed me back onto the mattress and straddled my upper chest. He pushed his painfully hard cock down and into my hungry mouth. I sucked him with all of my might. He held onto the headboard, readjusted his position, and then began to face-fuck me.

The angle wasn't the best and Marcus recognized that right away like the dominant he was. Crawling off of the bed, he pulled my head to the side edge and over before reinserting himself back into my mouth. Marcus held my hips in place as he leaned over me and drilled his cock back and forth.

This face-fuck was a sure sign of his dominance. Marcus Battle was marking his territory and establishing his rank as the alpha male in our relationship. Not that his position or territory needed to be established, but I wondered if he was making sure that I remembered this during the summer when we would be apart. I certainly would not ever forget it.

Marcus came in a huge flood of hot cum that I swallowed quickly, but was still unable to keep it all inside me, so it poured out of the corners of my mouth and onto the floor beside the bed. I hated the thought that I wouldn't be able to do this again for him for several months, but I tried to banish that thought from my head and stay in the moment.

"Shhhhiiiitttt!" Marcus hissed through clenched teeth as he fell over the edge of the cliff. His hips continued to drive his now-sensitive organ in and out of my velvety mouth, as almost on auto-pilot.

Finally, he stopped moving and slowly pulled his still hard cock out of my mouth. He looked down with satisfaction on his handsome face and gently slapped me on the cheek. "You are a fucking miracle worker, Loch."

"That was no miracle," I said with a laugh. I sat up on the bed, letting the blood rush out of my head and said, "It was a goddamn fantastic face-fucking by my own personal sex god."

Marcus laughed out loud and repeated my words, "Sex god . . ."

"Yes, sex god. Now, sex god, come over here and show me what you can do with this hole," I ordered him, my voice husky and full of lust. I lay down on the bed and lifted my legs onto my chest, fully exposing his favorite target.

"Mmmm! You are just asking for it, now," he growled.

"I'm so spoiled that I don't have to wait for you to recover. I don't know how I will ever survive the everyday ho-hum world without my sex god for a whole summer."

Marcus slapped a flat hand over my mouth, and in his most commanding voice, said, "Shut up! I don't want to think about that right now. I want to tear this fucking tight little chute up and not hear your fucking mouth."

I knew that he was playing a role and not upset with me, so I complied. Satisfying myself with teasing the palm of his hand, which he had kept covering my mouth with my tongue, I watched wide-eyed as he slid his reddened joint inside of my tight hole.

Groaning loudly into his palm, I squeezed my eyes shut and gutted through the pain. The flange of his cock head finally cleared my anal ring and I relaxed slightly before his thick shaft slid into me, holding me stretched to my limits.

"That's it, baby. You're treating this sex god right. Giving him just what he needs."

I arched my back as Marcus filled me with inch after inch of his throbbing manhood. His hand followed the arch, keeping my mouth clamped shut. When he reached the bottom of my well and I felt his pubic hairs tickling my ass cheeks, I knew that I was completely full of him. I was delirious for him to fuck me, but at the same time, I didn't want him to pull that magnificent piece of meat out of me either. I wanted it all. I wanted all of him. And he wanted all of me.

I got everything that I wanted, because Marcus gave me a really hard fucking and then kept his hard cock inside me before doing it all over again. We spent the next hour and a half, fucking and then relaxing with his pole never leaving my ass. It was magical and just what we both needed before the long separation.

"You're going to miss this," I said lazily. My head was lying on Marcus' sweaty chest as I sat in his lap. His cock was in my sloppy ass, throbbing away like a ticking time bomb to always make me aware of its presence. His arms were wrapped around my back, holding me to him. Marcus' back was propped against my headboard and I listened carefully to his heartbeat and breathing. I wanted to know everything about him.

"I know," he said simply. "You've completely spoiled me."

"Me?" I asked with a chortle.

He laughed easily. "I'm just giving you what you need . . . providing a service, so to speak."

"Some service." I snorted. "You should get some kind of gold star for your work ethic."

"Hhhmm, I think I'm getting the gold star right now."

"I'll say!" I exclaimed as I sat up and looked into his face. I was struck by the kindness and affection that it conveyed. Without even thinking, I reached up and touched Marcus' face. He had grown out his beard like I had asked him to and even though the dark copper hairs didn't completely fill in he looked older and more rugged, which was perfect for me.

"What are you doing?" Marcus asked, curiosity flavoring his voice. And to his credit, he didn't pull away from my hand.

"Memorizing your face," I answered as I continued to study his lips, his strong chin, his nose, his cute ears, his arched eyebrows, and his golden eyes.

"I didn't think it was my face that you liked . . ."

I followed his lips up and down with my fingers as he talked. "I like it very much. Not that we can't make some changes that would make it even better . . ."

"Oh yeah?" he chuckled. "Like what?"

I put my hands up into his sweat-soaked hair and brushed it to the side. "I don't know. Maybe a new hair style for your sophomore year . . ."

"And what new thing will you have for your sophomore year?" he asked, sarcasm dripping from his mouth.

"What would the great Marcus Battle like to change about me?" I asked with a smirk of my own.

"Not a thing. Not one single thing."

I laughed at his smile. "Now that you have these, there's nothing else?" Lifting my arms, I flexed my biceps and proudly showed him the results of all of my working out at his direction.

Marcus immediately put his hands on my biceps and squeezed them. I could feel his cock swell inside my tight chamber. "These *are* impressive."

"Let me see yours." I practically drooled waiting for him to flex.

He let go of my muscles and then flexed his own. I assumed the same position with him and squeezed his big biceps. "These have really gotten big."

"Nice, huh?"

"That's not the only thing that's gotten bigger," I growled as I ground my ass into his crotch.

Marcus reached down and grabbed each of my ass cheeks with his hands and spread them apart. "It's bigger and faster."

"Is it now?" I smirked.

We then showed each other how far we had come in a year. And it was only the end of the first year.

YOU MAY ALSO ENJOY THE FOLLOWING FROM EXTASY BOOKS INC:

Batting Cage
Crawford Rhine

Excerpt

The cage was large, for a cage. It had a hardwood floor and smooth bars. Smooth bars are a plus for a cage. You would be surprised how often you touch them when you are riding in a cage, like I was. I'm tall, over six feet and the cage actually allowed me to sit upright and I probably could squat, if I ever wanted to.

I had been travelling for what seemed like the better part of a day, so my best guess was that I was out West somewhere. Time was hard to tell because there was a heavy curtain over the cage that blotted out everything except for a rim of light at the bottom. It was hard to tell if the light was sunlight or artificial. I was grateful for the curtain since I was almost naked in the cage, wearing only a jockstrap. My eyes had become accustomed to the dark and I would occasionally hear voices, although I couldn't hear much of the conversations.

I did know that I had travelled by plane and now by truck of some sort. I could tell I was getting close to my destination, because I could hear the sounds of a city and noticed the stop and start of traffic. The air was hot, so that didn't help my guessing. It was summer, after all. I couldn't imagine having to be transported like this in cold weather. That would have been even more uncomfortable.

Then I was being unloaded by what sounded like a forklift. The familiar beeping when they went in reverse and the quick turns made me pretty sure I was right. I seemed to be going down a long hallway, bumping across doorways. Then a quick drop and I could hear cheering and male voices. I instantly felt nervous and thought I might throw up.

"Trent, what did you ask for?" asked a husky voice.

"I asked for an older, tall, white, smart, southern, professional, masculine, outgoing Servant with a happy personality," said the one that must be Trent. He clicked off these qualities like he had them memorized from a list.

"Why southern?" asked another voice.

"I want us to like the same foods, of course!" was Trent's response. He had a nice voice, even in timbre, deep and powerful. "Well, let's see how I did."

The curtain was pulled off and my body instantly took over. I rose to a squatting position on the balls of my feet with my legs spread in a V-shape, my arms on my upper legs and my head bowed. This position really exposed me, especially in this jockstrap with no back and a front that was basically a band with a basket of fabric suspended from it.

The room was silent, but I knew there were a lot of guys there. I could see we were indoors—the carpet was high quality and patterned in a red and white scheme. I could see the legs of a lot of wooden benches that looked like expensive furniture. I could also see the shoes and lower legs of the man I presumed was Trent.

He was wearing cleats and baseball pants, the kind that are white with a red pinstripe down the side. My mind was going a million miles an hour, and I guessed I was in the locker room of a baseball club. The cleats were dusty and there was dirt on the bottom of his white pants. His shoes were large, if I was guessing probably a size fourteen. His legs matched his feet in size, so it looked natural. I knew that he was sizing me up as well, and he had a much better view than I did.

I consider myself in pretty good shape, but squatting in that position was not comfortable and I could feel the strain in my legs. I had always had good leg muscles, even if I didn't go to the gym, ever. I guess this was just one of the reasons why Servants were usually much younger than me. I was already very tense, and now my twenty-nine-year-old muscles were letting me hear it. The silence and the wait were agonizing. I didn't know what was coming next or what to do when it came.

My thoughts were shattered by the view of a hand coming towards me through the bars. It was a big, beefy hand, and I could see the veins popping out on the back and running up his arm. He was beautifully tan and had blonde hair on his forearm. I had to fight the instinct to pull away from him, hard.

"Look at me." I felt his fingers under my chin at the same moment that he spoke. They were lifting my head up towards him. I kept my eyes down as my head raised but more and more of the scene was revealed to me as I went along. It was definitely a baseball locker room, the Los Angeles Angels, as a matter of fact. I was in Anaheim. There were probably ten other guys in the room standing in the background.

I didn't get a great look at him, but I could see that he was tall, even though he was squatting to look into the cage. His uniform hinted at a body that was very broad and muscled. When his fingers left my chin, I turned my eyes up to his face.

"Holy shit!" I thought to myself. It's Trent Parks. His face was boyishly round and he had that familiar sense of serenity about him that I had seen when watching him on TV. He was very handsome, and I was thrilled he was my Master. Our eyes locked onto each other, and I was held by his gaze.

"I am your Master, and I'm very glad that you are finally here. I want you to know that everything will be great and you have nothing to worry about." The speech was stilted like he had been practicing it, but I felt sincerity roll off of him and I felt myself relax inside. His voice was very reassuring, and I was hopeful that this first meeting was to be how he would treat me in the future.

"How was your trip?" he asked.

"It was in a cage . . . .Sir," I replied, pausing too long before the required title.

The room burst into laughter, and I feared that I had just blown it. I looked back into his eyes expecting to see anger, but instead his mouth was curled up in a small smile and his eyes were twinkling with delight. Once again, I was relieved and let myself breathe.

"We're going to have to find something to stuff in that mouth of yours later," Trent commented, more to his team-mates than to me, but I definitely heard it and comprehended his meaning. "I will see you later at home after my game."

The curtain was being dropped around the cage now, and I heard Trent giving instructions to the handlers for them to deliver me to his house and that his Dad would be there to let them in. He also asked them to make sure I was comfortable and fed.

With the curtain closed the guys talked freely like I could not hear them. Or maybe, it didn't matter that I could hear them.

"Well, Trent. Did you like him?"

"Is he what you pictured? Sometimes they don't get it right."

"He looked right to me!" This was followed by laughter. "He's a big boy!"

Then Trent's voice again, "He seems to be exactly what I wanted."

"He looks and sounds like he can give you a run for your money, Parks!"

"I hope so."

"What's the agreement that you made with The Service?"

"Standard. He works for a year and he can decide whether to continue for another year. If he does, he gets the whole payment, if he doesn't, he gets half."

I heard the forklift before I felt it underneath the floorboards of the cage and then we were moving. Being loaded back on the truck and heading to my new home.

ABOUT THE AUTHOR

This is Crawford's first book in his series, Cageless In College. He was inspired by a trip to the beautiful campus of the University of North Carolina to write a series based on a marked man who took a different path and attended college instead of going into The Service.

Crawford Rhine is easily inspired by travelling. His series The Romanian Chronicles was inspired by a summer trip to Romania and Russia where he completed four books and has added some since. These books are re-imaginings of the classic movie monsters from the 1930's, updated with new twists like Dracula, Frankenstein, the Werewolf, and the Phantom of the Opera. A recent trip to Switzerland provides the backdrop for the Invisible Man, still to be published.

Crawford's first series The Master & Servant Series are inspired by sports and occupations that traditionally exude masculinity like baseball, basketball, football, acting, and being a country music star. A trip to Denmark has inspired a book on soccer still to come.

He looks forward to continuing to travel to far-away places and publishing more books in each series.